A PEACEFUL RETIREMENT

A PEACEFUL RETIREMENT

MISS READ

ILLUSTRATIONS BY ANDREW DODDS

BCA

LONDON NEW YORK SYDNEY TORONTO

The edition published 1996 by BCA by arrangement with Michael Joseph

First published in Great Britain 1996
Copyright © Miss Read 1996
Illustrations copyright © Andrew Dodds 1996

Set in 11.5/13.5 pt Monotype Garamond
Typeset by Datix International Limited, Bungay, Suffolk
Printed in England by Clays Ltd, St Ives plc

A CIP catalogue record for this book is available from the British Library

CN 4460

The moral right of the author has been asserted

*To the happy memory of Beryl, Edie,
Anthea, Laura, and my sister Lil, whose
lives enriched my own*

Contents

1 A New Start

W<small>HEN</small> I retired, after many years as headmistress of Fairacre School, I received a great deal of advice.

The vicar, the Reverend Gerald Partridge, was particularly concerned.

'You must take care of your health. You have had to take early retirement because of these recent weaknesses, and you must call in the doctor if you are in any way worried.'

My assistant, Mrs Richards, was equally anxious about my welfare, and urged me to cook a substantial midday meal.

'I've seen so many women living alone who make do with a boiled egg, or even just a cup of tea and a biscuit. In the end, of course, they just fade away.'

Mr Willet, who is general caretaker at the school, as well as verger and sexton at the church, and right-hand man to us all at Fairacre, told me not to attempt any heavy digging in my garden at Beech Green. He would be along to see the vegetables planted, he assured me, and there was no need to try to help with the plans he had in mind.

Mrs Pringle, the morose school cleaner with whom I had skirmished for years, ran true to form.

'I'll be along on Wednesdays as usual,' she informed me,

'and don't try taking that great heavy vacuum cleaner upstairs. That way my auntie Elsie met her death. Not that she died outright, mind you. She lingered for weeks.'

It was the vicar again who had the last word, leaning into the car window, and saying earnestly:

'Everyone hopes that you will have a *really peaceful retirement*.'

I promised him that that was my firm intention too.

It had been a bitter blow to me when I had been obliged to retire a few years before my forty years of teaching were up. But once I had made up my mind I began to look forward to an easier way of life, and had comforted myself with all sorts of future plans when I should have the leisure to enjoy them.

I continued to look ahead joyfully, but I must admit that during the first day or two of that particular summer holiday, the beginning of my retirement, those words of advice, so kindly meant, gave me food for thought.

It seemed plain to me that the four people who had advised me so earnestly, really had a pretty poor view of my capabilities.

The vicar obviously considered that I was now a tottering invalid and incapable of looking after my own health.

Mrs Richards, who should have known better, seemed to think that I should neglect my digestion, sinking to scoffing the odd biscuit, and never making use of my cooking equipment.

I was rather hurt about this. I like cooking, and enjoy the fruits of my labours. What's more, I enjoy cooking for friends, and Mrs Richards had frequently had a meal at my house. Why should she imagine that one so fond of her food would suddenly give up?

As for Mr Willet, it was plain that he deplored my horticultural efforts, and was practically warning me off my own plot. What cheek!

Mrs Pringle's attack caused me no surprise. The threat of coming as usual every Wednesday 'to bottom me', as she so elegantly puts her ministrations, was expected, and her warning against lifting heavy objects, such as the vacuum cleaner, was only a request to keep from meddling with her equipment and damaging it.

Well, I thought, if the rest of Fairacre shared my advisers' opinions then it was a poor look-out for the future. I began to wonder if I should make early application for a place in an old people's home, but at that moment the telephone rang, and it was my old friend Amy's cheerful voice on the line.

*

Amy and I first met many years ago at a teachers' training college in Cambridge. We took to each other at once, although Amy, even then at the age of eighteen, had a worldly elegance which none of us could match. But with it she also had plenty of common sense, a kindly disposition and a great sense of humour. She was generally popular among the students of her own sex, and much sought after by the male undergraduates at Cambridge University.

We kept up our contacts when we were out in the world, and although Amy married within two years of our leaving college the friendship remained solid, and survived the union of James and Amy.

'What are you up to?' queried Amy.

I told her about my gloomy thoughts after receiving advice from old friends.

'Pooh!' said Amy. 'Pish-Tush, and all that! My advice is positive, not negative. Just you set to and enjoy your freedom. It's time you kicked up your heels, and did something exciting.'

'Good! I will!'

'Which reminds me. James has made the final arrangements for our week and a bit in Florence, at the end of September. It's all buttoned up. Air tickets, hotel and all that. I'll pop over one day soon and tell you more, and we can begin to make plans about what we girls are going to do while James is at his boring old conference.'

I was excited at the prospect. Amy had mentioned it earlier, but now this wonderful holiday was in sight.

I burbled my thanks and said I should look forward to seeing her at any time, as I was now a Free Woman.

I put down the receiver feeling considerably elated. A fig for my advisers!

*

Those first two or three weeks of my retirement were blissful. We were enjoying a spell of fair weather that summer, and downland is at its best then.

The garden was at its most colourful and fragrant. In the flower borders the pinks and cottage carnations scented the air during the day, and some tobacco plants added their own aroma as dusk fell. Mr Willet had experimented with a wigwam of bamboo sticks which was covered in sweet peas of all colours, and it was a joy to take my ease on my new garden seat, Fairacre's farewell present on my retirement, and to relish the delights about me.

I was filled with first-day's-holiday zeal, and washed and ironed curtains and bedspreads, rejoicing in the summer breezes which kept them billowing on the clothes-line. I turned out drawers and discovered enough rubbish to stock a dozen jumble stalls. This latter activity was accompanied by a commentary of self-accusation. Why did I buy that dreadful peacock-blue jumper? It was a colour I never wore. What on earth possessed me to spend good money on a mohair stole? I remember that the only time I wore it, to a Caxley concert, it had slithered from my shoulders half a dozen times, and had been retrieved by as many fellow listeners. It had so embarrassed me that it had been relegated to the bottom drawer with other jumble fodder such as too-small gloves, too-large petticoats and a variety of Christmas presents which I should never use.

It was a salutary task. I must take myself in hand, I told myself severely, and be much more selective in my shopping. After all, my income would be greatly reduced, and I must be more prudent.

Nevertheless, the feeling of achievement as I contemplated the tidy drawers did me a world of good, and added to my general contentment.

Of course, my domestic euphoria was dampened by the weekly visits of Mrs Pringle who enjoyed pointing out my shortcomings as she puffed about her duties on Wednesday afternoons. However, I was quite used to the old curmudgeon's strictures, and she brought me news of my Fairacre friends, which was most welcome.

I was particularly interested to hear how my old friend Henry Mawne was getting on with his new wife Deirdre. He had first come to Fairacre alone, and the village had been quite sure that he was a respectable bachelor, and it had been intrigued and delighted when he became most attentive to me. I did not share the general excitement, and found him rather a nuisance.

Fairacre's hopes of two middle-aged people tying the knot in the parish church of St Patrick's were abruptly shattered when Henry's wife reappeared. She had been staying with relatives in Ireland after the marriage had suffered a temporary set-back. My relief had been great.

The three of us became good friends and I was sad when she died. The new Mrs Mawne was one of her Irish relatives, and seemed to be generally approved of by the residents of Fairacre. But not, of course, by Mrs Pringle.

'For one thing,' she said, as we sipped tea, 'she talks funny. I don't take in one word in four.'

'I rather like that Irish brogue.'

My remark was ignored.

'And she's fair upset Bob Willet with all her fancy ideas for the garden.'

'What ideas?'

'A camomile lawn for one. Bob was fair taken aback by that. Takes years to settle he told her, and what was wrong with the grass lawn as had been there for years?'

'Will Bob do it?'

'Not likely. And she wanted Alice Willet to go up every evening and cook the evening meals. That didn't suit Bob nor Alice, as you can guess.'

I felt sorry for poor old Henry if his wife really was putting her foot in it so readily. However, one learns over the years to take Mrs Pringle's news with a pinch of salt, and I looked forward to hearing more from less rancorous sources.

'It's a great pity,' said Mrs Pringle, heaving herself upright ready for further onslaughts on my property, 'as he didn't look nearer home for a second wife. You'd have made him a good wife. Apart from the housework, of course.'

I was roused to protest.

'You know perfectly well that Mr Mawne and I had no sort of understanding. I certainly had no thoughts of entangling the man.'

The old harridan was quite unabashed.

'Which reminds me,' she said, 'how is your new friend Mr Jenkins getting on?'

I ignored the question, but she had scored a hit, and knew it.

John Jenkins was one of the problems I should have to face in my retirement. He was a most attractive middle-aged widower who had come to live in Beech Green quite close to my cottage.

We had become good friends, and shared a great many interests. We both liked walking, visiting splendid houses and gardens, attending plays and concerts, and enjoyed each other's company.

He had been lonely, I think, when he first arrived in Beech Green, and glad of my company. I was still busy at Fairacre school, and my time at home was pretty full with the usual woman's chores of cooking, laundering, writing letters and entertaining.

At times I found his presence tiresome. He was plainly at a loose end. I was not, but I tried to be a good neighbour and companion within my limits.

The awkward thing was that John soon wanted more of my time, and asked me to marry him. I refused, as kindly as I could.

However, he was not in the least dismayed, and continued to propose to me with admirable tenacity. But I was equally adamant, and a permanent, if uneasy, truce prevailed.

Amy, of course, was all in favour of marriage for me. Ever since her own union with James she has urged me to enter the state of matrimony, and produced a string of possible suitors over the years. I have been grateful to Amy for her well-meant endeavours on my behalf, but I have also been irritated. Time and time again, I have explained to my old friend that I am really quite happy as a spinster, but Amy simply cannot believe it.

'But you must be so lonely,' she protested one day. 'You come home from school to an empty house, so quiet you can hear the clock tick, no human voice! It must be almost frightening.'

'I don't,' I told her. 'I find it absolute bliss after the fuss and bustle of school. And I may not come back to human voices, but Tibby keeps up a pretty strong yowling until I put down her dinner plate.'

Amy was not impressed, and her attempts to provide me with a husband have continued unabated over the years.

This question of loneliness interests me. I remember when I made the move from Fairacre school house to my present home which dear Dolly Clare left me, that I had a brief moment when I wondered if I should really be at ease on my own.

At the school house I had been much nearer my neighbours, and in any case, the children and their parents were much in evidence around me. Certainly, at holiday times I had found the place much quieter, but this had pleased me.

After the move to Beech Green, and my passing doubts about loneliness, I found my new surroundings entirely satisfactory, and when I informed Amy that I was really and honestly not *lonely*, it was the plain truth.

I think perhaps those of us who have lived in a solitary state are lucky in that they have filled their time with a diversity of interests and friends. It is the married couples who suffer far more when their partner goes, for they have shared a life together, and it is shattered by the loss of half one's existence. Life for the one who is left can never be quite the same again.

I feel it would be heartless to share this thought with Amy. She is positive that she is the lucky one to be married, and I am to be pitied.

But I wonder . . .

I had taken very little notice of Mrs Pringle's strictures about Deirdre Mawne. I was so accustomed to her disparaging remarks about all and sundry that the Mawnes' marital affairs were dismissed from my mind.

However, when Bob Willet mentioned the matter, in his usual thoughtful and kindly manner, I began to take more notice.

He spoke about Mrs Mawne's invitation to Alice, his wife, to take a permanent job as their cook every evening at the Mawnes' house to provide dinner on a regular basis, weekends included.

'She offered to pay well,' said Bob fairly, 'but that's not the point. I'm not having Alice turning out in all weathers, and after dark too, best part of the year, to do a job as Mrs Mawne can quite well do herself. It's asking too much.'

I agreed.

'I don't know how they go on in Ireland,' continued Bob, putting four lumps of sugar in his mug and stirring briskly, 'but I should hope the folk there don't kowtow to the likes of Mrs Mawne. She won't find no slave labour in Fairacre. We ain't standing for her high and mighty ways, I can tell you.'

'She'll soon learn,' I said comfortingly.

'I'm not so sure. She's upset Mr Lamb at the village shop keeping him waiting for his money. She says she's always paid her bills monthly, but that's a long time for him to wait for the cash, and half the time he has to remind her because she's let it run on. People don't like having to do that. He's in a proper tizzy.'

Bob Willet himself was getting quite pink in the face as his account went on.

'And she's making trouble with the vicar,' he continued. 'Strode up the aisle to sit in the front pew where old Miss Parr always sat for years. She says that pew belongs to whoever has the house, which they do now, as you know, but no one ever took that pew after Miss Parr died. Mr Mawne always sat three rows back ever since he came to Fairacre.'

I rose to put my mug in the sink, hoping to bring this unhappy recital to a close. I had never seen the usually imperturbable Bob Willet so incensed.

'I'm sure it will all blow over,' I said hopefully. 'Henry Mawne knows all about village ways. He'll explain things to her.'

'If you ask me,' he said, putting his mug beside mine in the sink, and preparing to return to the garden, 'he's scared stiff of her.'

I heard him trundling out the lawn mower. He was singing *Onward Christian Soldiers*, which seemed, I thought, to suit his present martial mood.

I rinsed the mugs, feeling relieved that I no longer lived close to the Mawnes and their troubles. With any luck, I told myself, I should hear no more of the subject.

I should have known better.

The weather continued to be calm and sunny, and I pottered about my garden and the lanes of Beech Green in a state of blissful enjoyment. The thought that I need never go to school again filled me with satisfaction which, in a way, rather

surprised me for I had never disliked my job, and had certainly wondered if I should miss the hurly-burly of school life after so many years.

However, this halcyon period suited me admirably and I seemed to notice things which had escaped me before. I took to picking a few wild flowers from the banks and hedgerows on my daily strolls. I marvelled at the exquisite symmetry of the pale mauve scabious flowers and the darker knapweed that grow so prolifically in these parts.

There was a patch of toadflax just outside the wall of Beech Green's churchyard, and I enjoyed these miniature snap-dragons with their orange and yellow flowers, and the spiky leaves which set off their beauty so vividly.

It was one of these mornings, when I was mooning happily with a nosegay of wild flowers in my hand, that John Jenkins drew up alongside in his car and invited me to coffee. I accepted willingly and climbed in.

'You realize you are breaking the law, madam,' he said with mock severity, nodding at my flowers.

'It's all in the cause of botanical knowledge,' I told him. 'Have you been to Caxley?'

Our local market town on the river Cax serves many villages around, and there are still many people who go every market day for their shopping, despite one or two out-of-town supermarkets.

'Yes, I had to see my solicitor. Luckily he has a car park for clients at the rear of his office, otherwise I'd still be driving round and round the town looking for a parking place.'

'People shouldn't have cars,' I said.

'You mean *other people* shouldn't have cars,' he countered, turning into his drive.

Ten minutes later we were drinking proper coffee, expertly made, which put me to shame as I usually gave him instant.

'This luscious brew makes me feel guilty and weak,' I told him.

'Good,' he replied briskly. 'This might be a propitious time to suggest that you marry me. I promise to make the coffee in the years ahead.'

'No go,' I told him, 'but the coffee offer might have done the trick this time. By the way, I've been asked to take charge of the Sunday School here.'

'Oh dear, has George started already? I told him not to bother you.'

I felt slightly piqued by this. That John should institute himself as my protector was really a bit much. Anyone would think we were already married, and that I was incapable of looking after my own affairs.

'Well, George is not the only one, of course, to rush to enlist my invaluable services. But never fear! I realized that I should be pestered to join all sorts of things when I retired and I am determined to be firm.'

'I'm glad to hear it. Let me know if anyone starts to bully you, and I'll see them off.'

I put down my cup carefully. Mellowed though I was by his excellent coffee, I was not going to stand for this knight-to-the-rescue attitude.

'John,' I began, 'I'm not ungrateful, and you are one of the first people I should turn to in trouble, but I must point out that I have managed my own affairs – not very competently perhaps, but I've got by – for a good many years, and I am not going to start asking for help now. Unless, of course,' I added hastily, 'I am absolutely desperate.'

'What a prickly old besom you are,' commented John pleasantly, refilling my cup with a steady hand. 'You remind me of a hedgehog.'

I laughed.

'I like hedgehogs,' I told him.

'I like this one,' he assured me.

We drank from our replenished cups in relaxed and companionable silence.

2 Ponderings

THE EXPECTED rush of invitations to join this and that quickened its pace during early September, and I was asked to bestow my time and ability upon diverse activities, from arranging the flowers in Beech Green church to judging the entries of those local Brownies who were aspiring to a literary badge to wear on their sleeves.

The first invitation I turned down as politely as I could. I am one of the grasp-and-drop-in brigade of flower arrangers, and anything on a large pedestal involving great lumps of Oasis and hidden strings would be beyond me.

The Brownies could be undertaken in my own home and in my own time, and as hardly any of the little girls seemed to have literary aspirations, preferring very sensibly to opt for cooking or knitting, my judicial skills would not be over-worked. I took on this little chore with great pleasure.

I had the chance to be a secretary, a treasurer, a general ad-viser, a part-time librarian, a prison visitor, a baby-minder and a regular contributor to our local radio station.

'I can't think how they all got on without me,' I confessed to Amy one sunny September afternoon, as we sat in my garden.

'They must be jolly hard up,' said Amy. I thought this rather hurtful, but said nothing. 'I mean, your flower arrangements are pathetic, and I can't see you bringing any comfort to prisoners. You'd probably frighten the life out of them.'

'Well, I've turned those down anyway. I have put my services at the disposal of the hospital drivers.'

Amy looked alarmed.

'Not *ambulance* work surely? You know how you hate blood.'

'No, no. Of course not. I'm not qualified for anything like that. I've just offered to run people to hospital for treatment. George Annett asked me, and I'd turned down so many of his pleas to help at the church here, that I felt I had to say "Yes" to something.'

'It's always so difficult to refuse friends,' agreed Amy. 'My father always said: "Never do business with family or friends," and it was good advice.'

'Well, this isn't exactly *business*,' I began, but Amy interrupted me, with a wave of her long ivory cigarette-holder.

'Near enough. You're taking on responsibilities, and they'll be watching you to see if you can cope or not. Just be cautious, dear, that's all I'm advising.'

She spotted a butterfly on the lavender, and sauntered over to inspect it. I followed her.

'Stick to just one or two projects,' she continued. 'You are a bit like this creature, flitting here and there rather aimlessly.'

'Thank you, Amy! That's quite enough of your advice for one day! Still, it's nice to be compared to a butterfly. The last animal was a hedgehog.'

'And I bet that was dear John Jenkins' description,' said Amy shrewdly.

When Amy had gone I pondered on her words. I was feeling

rather bad about the Annetts. They were both old friends, and Isobel had been my assistant teacher at Fairacre school before she married George, the headmaster of Beech Green school.

My retirement, which brought me geographically so much closer to them, had made me more vulnerable to the demands on my time, as I had told Amy, from all those clubs, and so on, at Beech Green.

To my dismay, George Annett was among the most pressing in his demands, chiefly on behalf of his church.

He had been organist there for years, and at Fairacre's St Patrick's too. He was a zealous supporter of the church at Beech Green, and I was not surprised when he first made attempts to secure my services in one or more activities. But I did not want to commit myself. I might live now in the parish of Beech Green, I told him, but my inclinations and loyalties were towards the vicar and church at Fairacre.

'But you could do both,' he protested vehemently. 'There's no reason why you shouldn't attend Fairacre *and* Beech Green. The church is universal, after all.'

He was growing quite pink in his excitement, and Isobel intervened.

'She knows her own affairs best, George,' she said quietly. 'Don't *pester* her.'

He laughed, but I could see that he would return to the fray before long.

I spoke to Isobel privately, saying that I was sorry to be so adamant, but that I was conscious of having only a certain amount of time and energy, and I was determined to ration these precious commodities so that I could continue to enjoy an independent and healthy retirement.

She was understanding, but George, when Isobel was absent, I noticed, continued to solicit my help in various church affairs, so that, as I had told Amy, I had agreed to do some hospital-driving.

A sop to Cerberus, I told myself.

The day after Amy's visit I had to go to the doctor's surgery to check that all was well.

Since the alarming couple of strokes which had made me decide to retire a year or so earlier than I had intended, I had been given some tablets, which I did my best to remember to take, and otherwise pursued my ordinary way of life, except for a three-monthly check which my zealous doctor insisted on.

It was a perfect September morning, far too lovely to spend in a doctor's waiting-room. I had collected three pearly mushrooms from my lawn at breakfast time, and had great plans for an egg, bacon and mushroom supper.

The ancient plum tree was heavy with fruit which would soon have to be picked if the birds were not to rob me. A late crop of spinach, Bob Willet's pride and joy, was doing splendidly in the vegetable patch, and some fine bronze onions, their tops bent over neatly, were maturing in the sunshine.

As I drove to the surgery I passed a covey of young partridges running along the edge of the road. They rose with a whirring of wings above the hedge to take cover in Hundred Acre Field beyond.

Once, I thought, that great field would probably have been golden with stubble from the newly cut corn, and the partridges would have found all the food they wanted there. Nowadays, the field was ploughed and sown within days of the crop being harvested, and the partridges had to look desperately for their erstwhile natural fodder.

There were seven or eight people waiting when I arrived,

but no one I knew, which was a pity. I went to the small pile of magazines and wondered if an ancient *Horse and Hound* would be more to my taste than *Just Seventeen*. The only other periodical available was *Autocar*. Obviously, someone had been having a good sort-out of the usual women's magazines. I opted for *Autocar*, but it was heavy going for one ignorant of the combustion engine, and I welcomed the approach of a chubby toddler who left her mother and an older woman to greet me.

'Hello. How old are you?'

'Older than you are,' I said diplomatically, as all attention was now focused on us. 'And how old are *you*?' I asked, turning the tables neatly.

'Three. I shall be four next. Then five. Have you got a mummy?'

'Not now. I once had one.'

She returned to her mother and patted her knee.

'This is my mummy, and this is my granny.'

She banged the older woman's knee and beamed at me.

I smiled, and they smiled back.

Not content with this civility, the child proceeded to introduce everyone in turn, despite the mother's protests, and it was amusing to note the reaction of the embarrassed company.

The two men present simply ignored the introduction, studying their magazines with undue concentration. The women were more obliging.

A handsome, middle-aged woman, in the sort of knitted suit I am always seeking in vain, inclined her head towards the child's relatives and said: 'How do you do!' very clearly and politely. The others smiled nervously and looked apprehensive. Perhaps they thought that the child would drag them across the room for greater intimacies. Certainly, she looked determined enough to do so, but a head appeared round the door, and the grandmother, mother and child were summoned into the presence. Relief flooded the waiting room.

My routine took only a few minutes, and I found that I was getting quite blasé about that contraption that doctors wrap round your upper arm and blow up. At one time I was sure that I should be suffocated, although reason told me that my air passages were some distance from the point of operation. But as I had now survived several of these unpleasant ministrations, I was positively carefree when the band tightened. An old campaigner, I boasted silently to myself.

'Are you keeping busy?' he enquired, when the tests were over. 'You don't feel lonely or unwanted?'

'Fat chance of that,' I assured him, remembering all those requests for my time and attention.

'Oh, good,' he said, rather doubtfully, I thought. 'So many people find retirement a bit sad, you know.'

'Not me,' I replied firmly.

That evening John Jenkins rang. Could I help him?

'In what way?' I asked guardedly. With such a persistent suitor one needed to stay alert. One slip of the tongue and I might find myself committed to matrimony.

'Well, it's like this. I have an aged uncle, ninety-something, who is now in a nursing home near Winchester, and he wants to see me. I've said I'll take him out to lunch. Would you come too and give me moral support?'

'Of course. I'd love to.'

'It won't be easy. He's stone deaf, and always was pretty crabby, but he was good to my family when we had hard times. He paid my school fees for a couple of years, my mother told me, and I'd like to see the old boy again.'

'When are you thinking of going?'

'Next Tuesday, if you're free.'

A hasty study of the diary showed only the entry 'AMY?' and I knew that she would be delighted to postpone whatever we had provisionally planned if it meant any furtherance of romance for me, so I said I should look forward to the trip to the nursing home.

'Marvellous! What an angel you are! I warn you that you will be as hoarse as a crow and utterly exhausted after a couple of hours with Uncle Sam.'

'I'll cope,' I said.

'I'll bring you back to my house for a refreshing cup of Earl Grey and a slice of your favourite Battenburg cake.'

'Balmoral, isn't it? It got its name changed during the war.'

'Really? How erudite you are. Anyway, we always called it "window cake" in our youth, so you can take your pick. You do still like it?' he added anxiously.

'I do indeed,' I told him, and rang off. Now, what to wear when one visited a very old gentleman in a nursing home?

By Tuesday the weather had changed. The sky was dark with racing clouds rushing from the Bristol Channel to East Anglia.

I had put on a light-weight jersey dress with long sleeves, but brought a good thick cardigan with me. The fashion magazines are constantly telling their readers that: 'Cardigans are *out*', but not in Beech Green, I should like to tell them.

The windscreen wipers were active all the way, but it was warm in the car, and John and I enjoyed a lively conversation about the merits of nursing homes we had known, and which we should choose when the time came. Although the topic was a solemn one, we became mildly hilarious over our choice, and the journey passed happily.

Uncle Sam's nursing home lay half a mile from the road, and was an imposing building of Palladian design, set among well-tended gardens ablaze with dahlias and Michaelmas daisies. There were several white garden seats at strategic points, but these were dripping with raindrops as we emerged from the car, and naturally were unoccupied.

John's uncle was waiting for us in the hall. He was an imposing figure, tall and upright despite his ninety-odd years, and with a loud booming voice. He shook my hand with enormous vigour when we were introduced and offered us drinks which we declined.

'Let's get straight off to your local,' suggested John. I think he felt ill at ease in this very hot building with one or two occupants passing by on their walking frames or sticks.

We helped the old gentleman into an enormous raincoat, found his stick, cap and scarf and ushered him down the three steps to the car. Luckily the rain was ceasing.

As Uncle Sam and John were in the front, I could relax at the back and let their conversation take over. I began to understand why John had warned me about the old man's deafness. If John spoke, his uncle boomed: 'What? What?' and John was obliged to shout back. Uncle Sam himself spoke with a voice which would have carried across the Albert Hall. I began to wish I had brought some cotton-wool with me to stuff in my ears.

The bar of Uncle Sam's choice was warm and welcoming. He plumped for whisky and soda, and John and I sipped sherry. After studying menus so large that they really needed a lectern to support them, we all decided to have 'Today's Special', which was roast turkey with all the trimmings, and sat back with our duty done to enjoy each other's company.

I said that I was most impressed with the nursing home, and was he well looked after?

'Too dam' well,' he bawled. 'Blasted nurses always watching you. Go through the drawers to see if you've got a bottle there.'

'And have you?' said John.

'What? What? Don't mumble, boy.'

'Do they find a bottle?' yelled John.

'No need to shout, I'm not deaf. It's just that you young people mumble so these days. Yes, sometimes nursie finds a bottle. Friends bring me one from time to time. I'm allowed a drop sometimes.'

He fingered his empty glass, but John did not respond. A

waiter appeared to summon us to the dining room, and we went in.

It was only half full and I remembered Amy telling me that: 'Lunch these days is really a non-event, except at business conferences.' Perhaps she was right, I thought, looking about me.

A middle-aged couple were at the next table and I recognized them as people I had met at a fund-raising party in Caxley. He was a minister at one of the town's churches. Baptist, if I remembered rightly. They looked briefly at us, but obviously did not recognize me. I was rather relieved, and hoped that Uncle Sam's remarks, delivered fortissimo, would not disconcert them.

'You thinking of marrying young John here?' he boomed.

'No indeed,' I said.

'Not yet, but later,' John said, at the same time. We exchanged amused glances.

'You don't want to get entangled with our family,' he continued, attacking his asparagus soup with relish. 'Hard drinkers, and womanizers too.'

I was conscious of the attention of the minister and his wife.

'That's not true,' said John.

'What? What? Speak up, boy. Why, my brother Ernest got through two bottles of rum a day, and three wives. No, I tell a lie. *Four* wives, counting that flibbertigibbet that called herself a masseuse, and out-lived him.'

I noticed that the minister had cleared his plate rather quickly, and was asking the waiter for the sweet list. His face was somewhat flushed, although his glass had only been filled from the Perrier bottle on the table.

'Are there many other residents at the nursing home?' I enquired loudly.

'Forty, I believe. Don't see a lot of them. Mostly old women. Want to play cards for pennies, and I like high stakes myself. Always was a betting man, specially on the horses.'

Our turkey arrived and about half a dozen dishes with various vegetables, gravy and cranberry sauce. At the next table a waiter was setting plates of trifle before our neighbours.

'No, I shouldn't marry John here,' continued Uncle Sam. 'Not a good choice. Besides drink and women, there's a lot of nasty diseases in our family. That cousin of ours, lived near Portsmouth. Naval chap, remember him?'

He turned to John. He had dropped a large dollop of cranberry sauce down his shirt and I wondered if I should do some repair work.

'I don't think I knew a naval cousin,' said John.

'What? What? You must remember him. He was always picking up some foul disease abroad. Had rows of bottles on his wash stand. Can't think of his name, at the moment.'

The minister at the next table beckoned the waiter over.

'We will have coffee in the drawing-room,' he said firmly. 'Pray bring the bill there.'

He helped his wife from the chair, and they passed with dignity into the adjoining room.

If ever backs could register disapproval, theirs did. Frankly, I should have liked to join them.

Uncle Sam tackled apple pie and cream while John and I, replete and exhausted, watched him. John insisted on having coffee at the table, no doubt mindful of the minister and his wife recovering in the next room.

By the time our meal was over, there was a watery spell of

sunshine, and John suggested a drive before taking the old gentleman back to the nursing home.

'Splendid idea! Let's go and look at the race-course. It's years since I saw it.'

And so we drove some miles to the windy downs. By now Uncle Sam was quieter, content to watch the countryside and the trees beginning already to show signs of autumn.

There was a wide grass verge overlooking the race course, and here he insisted on getting out. He was very unsteady on his feet, but he seemed pleased to stand there, supported by John and me, while he relished the view before him.

The sun was out now, and great clouds threw their scurrying shadows across the grass. We all breathed deeply the exhilarating downland air, but it was chilly, and we soon returned to the car.

I think that secretly Uncle Sam was content to get back to the warmth and safety of the nursing home. He was beginning to look tired, and although he begged us, at the top of his voice, to stay for the rest of the day, we excused ourselves and made our farewells.

He shook hands energetically with John and took me into his arms to implant a very messy wet kiss on both cheeks. I was rather touched at such exuberance in a ninety-year-old.

A nurse appeared and took his arm.

'Now, Mr Jenkins, you've had a lovely outing and now it's time for your blood pressure pill.'

We watched the pair making for the lift, and then turned away.

'What a darling,' I said.

'I could do with a blood pressure pill myself,' observed John. 'What about you?'

'I think that cup of tea is more my mark,' I told him, as we pointed the car towards Beech Green.

*

We were quiet on the way home, not only because we were tired, but I think we were both dwelling on the problems of old age. The home was lovely, even luxurious, and the staff obviously dedicated and efficient. And yet it was sad.

I remembered the white hair, the frail limbs, the shaking heads, the walking frames and the distant bells ringing for help.

It was good to reach John's house, and to see that tea was already set out on a low table by the fireplace.

Soon he appeared with the teapot and the promised Battenburg cake, and we began to be more cheerful.

He insisted on running me home, and gave me a farewell

kiss as he drew up at my gate. It was, I noticed, much more acceptable than his uncle's.

'Thank you, my darling, for being such a support today. I suppose you couldn't make that a permanent part of your life?'

'Not really,' I said as kindly as I could, as I climbed out of the car. 'But thank you all the same for the nice thought, and the outing, and that perfect tea.'

He drove off looking, I thought, remarkably cheerful for an oft-rejected suitor.

3   Italian Interlude

THE LONG-AWAITED visit to Florence with Amy and James lay only three days ahead, and I had packed and unpacked my case at least five times to include or reject some item or other of my luggage.

Should I need a swimsuit? Unlikely, I decided, removing it. On the other hand, the pool was supposed to be a major attraction of the hotel. Perhaps? I put it back.

This sort of wavering went on for several days, and was most exhausting. I know that seasoned travellers simply pop in their essentials in twenty minutes flat, but I am not a seasoned traveller and, in any case, I like to be prepared for any eventuality. Air travel has made things worse for people like me. I might have been all right in Victorian times with a string of bearers humping a dozen or so pieces of my baggage on their heads. How simple it would have been to shout: 'Hey, could you put this hip bath on the last man's back?'

The evening before our departure I checked the case yet again, and also the contents of my small hand-case and handbag.

Domestic arrangements such as leaving keys and enough food for the cat – actually enough for three cats – had been made with kind Isobel Annett, who had also promised to report any such mishaps as burglary, fire or flood to the appropriate authority in my absence.

Mrs Pringle had insisted on coming for her usual Wednesday cleaning session, although I had begged her to have that day off.

'I won't hear of it,' she informed me. 'Miss one week in a place like yours, and there would be too much to cope with come the next Wednesday.'

I pointed out that there would be nobody in the house to make it dirty.

'What about that cat, traipsing in and out with mud on all four paws? What about any rats or mice he might see fit to bring and let lie *rotting* on the carpet? Then there's flies and wasps at this time of the year, not to mention birds as fly down the chimney.'

I gave in before this picture of my home as a teeming menagerie. As usual, Mrs P. had triumphed.

I had decided to go to bed early. We were to start for the airport at the civilized hour of 9 a.m., but I felt it wise to have a good night.

At half-past eight, as the sunset turned everything to gold, someone rapped at the front door.

On opening it, I saw to my dismay, that it was Henry Mawne, and he was looking singularly unhappy.

'Do come in, Henry,' I said. I should like to have added: 'But don't stay long,' but common civility restrained me.

He settled down in an armchair as though intending to stay for hours, and accepted whisky and water with a wan smile.

'Anything wrong, Henry?' I enquired. I hoped my tone was sympathetic. I was really trying to hurry the visit along so that I could get to bed early.

'*Everything*!' sighed Henry.

This did not bode well for my early-bed plans, but I made suitably dismayed noises.

'It's Deidre, she's pushed off.'

So the rumours had been right, I thought. In a village they usually are, but what could be done?

'She's bound to come back,' I said.

'I don't want her back,' replied Henry petulantly. He sounded like a four-year-old rejecting rice pudding.

'What went wrong?' It was best to get on with the story, I felt.

'*Everything*,' said Henry again. 'I should never have married her.'

He cast me a look so maudlin that I felt some alarm. For pity's sake, I thought, let me be spared another man needing my attention! I have neither the looks nor the temperament to set up as a *femme fatale*, so it did seem rather tough to have silly old Henry making sheep's eyes, especially when I needed a little peace.

'She's a very selfish woman,' said Henry. 'She never thinks about my side of things. Take breakfast, for instance.'

Should I be up in time to get mine, I wondered?

'I like a cooked one, bacon, eggs, sausage, you know what I mean. Deidre has a couple of slices of that straw bread with marmalade. I don't mind her having it, but why shouldn't I have what I want?'

'Do you cook it?'

He looked flabbergasted.

'Of course not. Old Mrs Collins always cooked it when I lived alone, before she started the housework. And that's another thing. She cut down Mrs Collins' hours, so she comes from ten until twelve.'

'Well, I expect she can manage with less help,' I said diplomatically. 'Your house always looks immaculate.'

'And she spends money like water,' continued Henry, swirling the contents of his glass moodily. 'Ordered a revolving summer house the other day. I put a stop to that, I can tell you. That's what really brought things to a head.'

'I'm sorry about this, Henry,' I said briskly, 'but there's really nothing that I can do. You and Deidre must sort it out. You've both got plenty of sense.'

'I wondered if you could speak to her for me? I've got her phone number.'

What a nerve, I thought!

'Henry, I shouldn't dream of coming between husband and

wife. In any case, I'm going away tomorrow.'

'Oh dear, that's most upsetting. I was relying on you.'

I began to get really cross. The selfishness of the man!

'I'm off to Florence, first thing.'

'How lovely! And such a short flight!'

He settled back in his chair, and held up his empty glass questioningly.

I took it and put it firmly on the table. Henry looked surprised.

'I'm certainly looking forward to the break,' I told him, 'but I've some packing to do now, and I'm going to turn you out.'

He rose reluctantly.

'I'm sorry if I've held you up.' He sounded huffy. 'You see, you are always the first person I think of when I'm in trouble. You mean so much to me.'

'Thank you, Henry, but this time things are different. You must get in touch with Deidre as soon as possible, and get her back. I'm sure you will be able to put things right between you.'

I opened the front door, and Henry paused. For one moment, I feared he was about to kiss me, but he thought better of it.

'Well, I hope you enjoy Florence,' he said wistfully. 'I wish I were coming with you.'

He set off down the path, his back registering the fact that he was a broken and misunderstood man.

I waved cheerfully as he unlocked his car, and then closed my door with great relief.

Come with me indeed! It would be good to be free of him for a blessed week.

Prompt as ever, James arrived in the car the next morning, and carried my case down the path while I locked up.

I bade farewell to Tibby who was too busy washing an elegantly outstretched leg to respond, and followed James to the car.

It was a blissfully sunny morning. The early mist had cleared, and the sun shone from a pale blue sky. All three of us were in great spirits.

We had no difficulty in getting to the airport and, having left the car in the long-term car park, James coped with all the necessary formalities, while we two pampered women went to see what the bookstall had to offer.

The magazine section displayed rows of journals most of them with covers showing bosoms and bottoms in highly uncomfortable attitudes. Some of the ladies were embellished with chains and whips, and the males adopted aggressive attitudes, unless they were entwined in passionate embraces with nubile females.

Amy studied the display with distaste.

'I really cannot fathom today's hysterical obsession with sex,' she remarked. 'One would think it was an entirely new activity.'

She selected *Homes and Gardens*, and I contented myself with the *Daily Telegraph* so that I could tackle the crosswords.

James joined us and surveyed the matter on offer.

'Good grief!' was his comment. 'I thought people grew out of that by fifteen. Where's the *Financial Times*?'

'Is the plane going to be on time?' asked Amy as we turned away.

'Only forty-five minutes late,' said James.

'Not bad at all,' replied Amy indulgently. 'What about a cup of coffee?'

My first impression of Florence was of all-pervading golden warmth. The buildings, the walls, the pavements, and the already changing colour of the trees from green to gold, gave the lovely city an ambience which enfolded one immediately.

Our hotel was in the oldest part of the city, not far from the Duomo, Florence's cathedral called so prettily Santa Maria del Fiore. The magnificent dome could be glimpsed, it seemed, from every quarter of Florence.

The hotel had once been the property of a wealthy Florentine family. The taxi driver whirled round the innumerable corners into ever more narrowing streets and at last pulled up with a flourish at an imposing doorway.

'I'm thankful I shan't have to do much driving in this place,' remarked James, as we alighted.

The taxi driver grinned.

'One way! Always one way!' He held up a nicotine-stained finger to add point, and then went to help James unload.

It was cool inside the building in contrast to the heat of the streets. The thick walls and small windows had been built to keep out the weather and had done so now for three centuries.

James and Amy were escorted into their room first, and I was ushered down a corridor to an attractive single room which overlooked the little garden.

It was an unremarkable patch, consisting mainly of some rough grass and shrubs, but my eye was immediately caught by the happenings in an adjoining garden.

A long clothes-line was almost filled with flapping white sheets, and two nuns were engrossed in unpegging them and folding them very tidily and exactly. They held the corners with their arms spread wide and then advanced towards each other, as if treading some stately dance, to fold the sheets in halves, then into quarters until there was a snowy oblong which they put on a mounting pile on the grass.

In contrast to their measured ritual of folding, and their solemn black habits and veils, their faces were animated. They smiled and gossiped as they worked. It was a happy harmony of mind and body, and a joy to watch.

We were more than ready for our evening meal when the time came, and the food was delicious, a precursor of all those we enjoyed at the hotel.

Later, we took a walk round the nearest streets, mainly for James to find the way from the front of the hotel to its car park at the rear.

Although he himself would have very little time for exploring, he had hired a small Fiat, to be delivered in the morning, so that Amy and I could do so.

'Do you know,' he exclaimed when he met us later at the hotel, 'it is exactly three-quarters of a mile from the front door to the hotel car park.'

'It can't be!' protested Amy. 'It's only at the end of the garden.'

'One way streets,' replied James, holding up a finger just as the taxi driver had done. 'Always one way!'

James was picked up each morning at nine o'clock. Two other men who were attending the conference were already in the car when it arrived, and we knew we should not see James again, most days, until the evening.

Amy and I found each day falling into a very pleasant pattern. After James' departure to work, we took a stroll to one of the famous places we had been looking forward to visiting for so long.

We soon discovered that there was enough to relish in the Duomo, Santa Croce and the Uffizi, to keep us engrossed for years rather than our meagre allotment of days available. But we wandered about these lovely buildings, and many others, for about two hours each morning when, satiated with art and history, we would sit in one of the piazzas and refresh ourselves with coffee.

After that we would return to the hotel, shopping on the way at a remarkable cheese shop. Here, it seemed, all the cheeses of the world were displayed. While we waited, and wondered at the riches around us, we looked at a line which ran across one wall of the whitewashed shop. It was only a few inches from the ceiling and marked how high the water had reached during devastating floods some years earlier. The proprietor told us about this with much hand-waving and eye-rolling, and although we had no words in common we had no doubt about the horrors the citizens of Florence had endured.

We purchased warm rolls nearby and delicious downy peaches, and thus equipped for a picnic lunch we went to fetch the car.

We made for the hills usually, visiting a cousin of Amy's mother's in Fiesole on one occasion, but falling in love with Vallombrosa we often pointed the car to that delectable spot which was just as leafy on those golden September afternoons as Milton described it so long ago in *Paradise Lost.*

> *Thick as Autumnal Leaves that strow the Brooks*
> *In Vallombrosa, where th'Etrurian shades*
> *High overarch't embow'r . . .*

Under the arching trees which sheltered us from the noon-day sun, we sat in companionable silence enjoying the quietness around us and the bread and cheese in our laps.

Later, bemused with Italian sunshine and beauty, we would head back to the hotel. Amy negotiated the one-way maze of streets to bring us successfully to the garage at the back of the hotel.

We walked through the shady and shaggy garden into the dim coolness, there to refresh ourselves with tea, before bathing and changing and settling down to await James's return from his labours.

I think I grew closer to Amy in those few magical days than at any other time in our long friendship. It may have been because we were alone together, in a foreign place, for most of the day, without the sort of interruption that occurs in one's home. No callers, no telephone ringing, no cooking pot needing attention, no intrusive animals interrupting our conversation or our quiet meditation.

We hardly spoke about home, although I did tell her one day, in the quiet shade of Vallombrosa, about Henry's unwelcome visit on the eve of our departure.

I was surprised at her reaction. Normally, when she hears that any man has visited me or taken me out, Amy responds with much enthusiasm, imagining that at last romance has entered my bleak spinster's life.

This time, however, she was unusually censorious of Henry's behaviour.

'Henry Mawne,' she began severely, 'has made his bed and must lie on it.'

'You sound like my mother,' I protested.

'Your mother had plenty of sense,' replied Amy. 'Really, Henry should know better than try to engage your sympathy.'

'He didn't.'

'He's chosen *two* wives,' went on Amy, 'and doesn't seem to have made either very happy. I can't feel sorry for him, and I hope you aren't.'

I reassured her on this point.

'It'll all blow over,' I said, 'once Deidre comes back.'

'But suppose she doesn't?'

'I think she will,' I said slowly.

'You don't sound very sure about it,' commented Amy. 'I should nip any advances of Henry's in the bud. I shouldn't like to see you with a broken heart.'

'A flinty old heart like mine doesn't crack very easily,' I said, and at that moment James appeared, looking remarkably buoyant for one who had been engaged in high-powered discussions on international trade and finance.

The time passed in a golden haze. Florence was still basking in the sunlight, like a contented cat, as we went by taxi to the airport.

Our luggage had grown since our arrival, as Amy and I had succumbed to temptation and bought soft Italian leather handbags, wallets and purses and a pair of glamorous shoes apiece. The range of beautiful silk scarves, which we had also acquired, would be so useful for Christmas presents we told each other, but I had no doubt that we should see them being worn by ourselves in the future.

It was raining when we alighted from the plane, and people were striding about in dripping raincoats. I was surprised to feel that somehow this was absolutely right. It was home-like, familiar and reassuring. Even the smell of wet tarmac and petrol fumes was welcoming.

James dropped me at my door, propping my luggage in the porch and promising to ring during the evening. I tried to thank him, but he brushed aside my endeavours with a great hug and a kiss.

Tibby, asleep on the stairs, opened a bleary eye, closed it again and went back to sleep.

In the kitchen a piece of paper, anchored to the table by the flour-dredger, was covered in Mrs Pringle's handwriting. It said:

Am out of Brasso. Washer gone on cold bath tap. Mouse come out from under the stairs. And went back.
See you Wednesday. M.P.

I was home all right.

4   Home Again

IT WAS good to be back.

I relished the cool air, the green countryside, my own goods and chattels, and best of all my comfortable bed.

In those first few days of my return, I realized how much my habitual surroundings meant to me. I looked anew upon morning dew on the lawn, on the yellowing poplar leaves fluttering and turning in the autumn sunshine, and the bright beads of bryony, red, orange and green, strung along the hedgerows. I had returned with fresh eyes.

I had also returned much stronger in body. The sunshine, the lovely food and the warm companionship of dear Amy and James had relaxed earlier tensions, and I had thrived in these perfect conditions.

But, even more important, was the nourishment of spirit which would sustain me for months, and probably years, to come. Constantly, as I went about my everyday duties, cleaning, cooking, gardening and the like, pictures came to mind; a glimpse of nuns folding washing, a sunlit alley, a barrowload of peaches under a striped awning, Donatello's David with his girlish hat and curls, or the plumes of water flashing from the fountains of Florence.

These exhilarating memories and hundreds more would, I knew, *'flash upon the inward eye'* for the rest of my life.

Mrs Pringle, when she came on Wednesday, commented on my improved appearance.

'Done you a power of good,' she informed me. 'I said to Alice Willet before you set off: "She's aged a lot since those funny turns. You could never had said she was *good-looking*, but she used to look *healthy*, but even that's gone."'

'Thanks,' I said.

'Funny how people's looks change. Mr Mawne now, he looks a real wreck since his wife left him.'

'Isn't she back yet?' I asked, feeling some alarm.

'We all reckon she's gone for good,' replied Mrs Pringle, with much satisfaction. 'He's not an easy man to live with. Still got a bit of that military business about him. He used to criticize his wife something dreadful.'

'The bedroom windows could do with a clean,' I said pointedly.

Mrs Pringle went to fetch appropriate cloths, and made her way upstairs. Her limp was unusually pronounced and her breathing unusually heavy, but I ignored these signs of umbrage and went out into the garden.

I found Mrs Pringle's news irritating. Should I have to put up with Henry's unwelcome visits? Surely he would have the sense to realize that his marital affairs were no business of mine. I was genuinely sorry for him, but saw only too well what a nuisance he could be.

And what about John Jenkins? I remembered, with misgiving, his offer to see off anyone who molested me. The thought of two middle-aged men coming to blows over a middle-aged spinster – not even good-looking – was too silly to contemplate, and I resolutely set to and attacked a riot of chickweed in the flower border.

A few days after my return from Florence I peeled September from the various calendars around the cottage and faced October. About time I sent off those Christmas parcels to New Zealand and Australia, I thought, with my annual shock.

Usually, I miss the last surface mail date, and have to cudgel my brains for something light enough to be sent by air mail. My overseas friends must be heartily sick of silk scarves and compact discs. This year I would be in time, I promised myself, and send boxes of soap, or books, or even delicacies such as Carlsbad plums.

Thus full of good intentions and armed with a shopping list, I drove into Caxley one morning and parked behind the town's premier store.

I visited the hosiery department first to stock up for the months ahead. There was so much choice it was formidable. Having made sure that I was looking at 'TIGHTS' and not 'STOCKINGS', the first hazard, I then had to find my way among the 'DENIERS'. After that, already wilting, I had to decide on 'COLOUR'. Why do hosiery manufacturers give their wares such extraordinary names? Who can tell what one can expect from 'Carribbean Sand' or 'Summer Haze'? A few leave a minute square of mica showing the contents, but short of taking the box to the door and using a magnifying glass whilst there, it is really impossible to judge.

However, I plumped for three pairs of 'Spring Hare' and three of 'Autumn Night' and then went to inspect the boxes of soap for my distant friends.

I must say, the display was magnificent and I selected six fragrant boxes for presents and for myself.

Smug with my success I chattered away to the obliging assistant about catching the surface mail for Christmas. She looked up from her wrapping with dismay.

'But they will weigh so much,' she protested. 'Why don't you buy something like handkerchiefs or scarves?'

It was rather deflating, but I rallied well.

'They've all had hankies and scarves,' I assured her. 'Besides, I shall feel really efficient catching the right post this year.'

The weather now changed. It grew chilly in the evenings and Tibby and I enjoyed a log fire.

It was sad to see summer fading. The trees had turned to varying shades of gold, and the flowers in the border were looking jaded. Soon we should get frosts which would dull their bright colours, and start the fall of leaves.

But there were compensations. My cottage was particularly snug under its thatch in cold weather. The walls were thick, the windows small by comparison with modern houses, but those men who had built it so long ago knew what downland weather could be in these exposed parts, and designed their habitations accordingly.

One October afternoon Bob Willet decided to have a bonfire of all the dead weeds, hedge clippings and some rotten wood from an ailing plum tree which he had pruned, I thought, with an unnecessarily heavy hand.

'Do that ol' tree a world of good,' he told me as I watched the smoke rising. He had a great pile of debris standing at the side of the incinerator, and forked loads into it with great vigour.

'What's the news?' I asked him. 'And where's Joe today?'

Joseph Coggs, one of my erstwhile pupils, often accompanies Bob when he comes gardening. I had made a round of gingerbread that morning with Joe in mind, but I had no doubt that Bob Willet would make inroads into my confection with the same energy that he was showing with the tending of the bonfire.

'Maud Pringle's leg's bad again on account of Miss Summers' telling her the stoves might have to be lit early.'

'Oh, that's old hat!' I said. 'Nothing new to report?'

He gave me a swift look.

'Nothing about Mrs Mawne so far. Mr Mawne goes about lookin' a bit hang-dog, but Mr Lamb said he'd squared up the account at the shop, so he's relieved, I can tell you.'

'She's bound to come back,' I said, with as much conviction as I could muster.

Bob threw a fresh forkful on to the crackling blaze. There was a pungent smell of burning ivy leaves and dried grass.

'It's a real whiff of autumn,' I said, trying to change the subject. But Bob was not to be deflected.

'They say she's sweet on some chap in Ireland. A cousin or something. I must say, there seem to be a rare lot of cousins in Ireland. I wonder why that is?'

'Well, the population's fairly small,' I said weakly, 'and they seem to have large families, so I suppose there would be a good many cousins.'

I was more shocked than I wanted Bob Willet to know about the possibility of Deidre settling for good in Ireland. Surely Henry would have enough spunk to go and fetch his wife back?

'And young Joe's been to a practice match in Caxley this afternoon. Some junior football league he was rabbiting on about. I can't see him being picked, but I give him the bus fare and wished him luck.'

'Good for you,' I said, glad to get away from the Mawnes' troubles. 'You'll have to eat his share of the gingerbread.'

'You bet I'll do that,' said Bob heartily, and threw on another forkload.

As with all village rumours, once you have heard it from one source you can be sure of hearing it from a dozen more.

It was Gerald Partridge, vicar of Fairacre, who was my next informant. He had called to give me the parish magazine and seemed content to sit and chat.

'Henry is not himself, you know,' he said sadly. 'Seems to take no interest in the church accounts or anything else at the moment. There's some talk of Deidre having an attachment at her old home. I sincerely hope it is only rumour. It would break Henry's heart to lose a second wife.'

'What's gone wrong do you think?'

The vicar looked troubled.

'Something the lawyers call "incompatability of temperament", I suspect. She's very vague in her outlook to everything,
and it upsets Henry who is really a very downright sort of person.'

Tibby chose this moment to leap upon the vicar's knees.
Gerald Partridge began to stroke the animal in an absent-
minded manner.

'Primarily, I think it's money,' he went on. 'Henry is not a
rich man, and I suspect that Deidre thought that he was when
she married him.'

'I must admit that I always thought that he was comfortably
off.'

'He has a pension, and he has that large house Miss Parr left
him. He gets a certain amount from renting out part of it, as
you know, but the place really needs refurbishing, and Henry
showed me some estimates for repairing the roof and rewiring
the whole place, and I must say that I was appalled. I forget
how much it was – I have no head for figures – but there were
a great many noughts. It was quite as frightening as some of
the estimates we get in for work on the church.'

'I shouldn't have thought Deidre was extravagant,' I said,
remembering her somewhat dowdy clothes and the complete
lack of entertaining which had been a source of complaint
from other ladies in the parish.

'She bets,' said the vicar. 'On horses.'

'I'd no idea she went to the races.'

'She doesn't. She sits by the telephone and watches the races
on TV, or reads the racing news in the paper. I believe a lot of
people do it.'

'Well, I must say it sounds more comfortable,' I replied. The
vicar looked unhappy, and rose to his feet, tipping the out-
raged cat on to the hearthrug.

At the door he paused.

'Poor Henry! Do be particularly nice to him, my dear, he is under great stress.'

Mrs Pringle also told me about Henry Mawne's afflictions, but with less Christian forbearance.

'They're man and wife and should keep them only unto each other like the Prayer Book says. I know she's no right to carry on in Ireland with this cousin of hers, but what's Mr Mawne been up to letting her go like that? He should be looking after her, for better or worse, like he vowed to do.'

There was no point in arguing with Mrs Pringle when she was in this militant mood, and I cravenly retreated to the garden on this occasion.

George and Isobel Annett both enquired about Henry's predicament and asked if it were true that his wife had left him.

When John Jenkins rang up that evening I was quite prepared to cut short any discussion of Henry's affairs, of which I was heartily sick.

To my surprise he made no mention of Henry, but simply told me that Uncle Sam had died suddenly, and the funeral was next week.

It was a shock. Although he was obviously frail, and I remembered vividly helping John to support the old man against the downland wind, he had seemed so alert, so energetic, and game for years to come.

'I am truly sorry, John. He was a dear, and I'm glad I met him. We had a lovely day together, didn't we?'

'You made that day for him.'

He hesitated and then said:

'I don't know how you feel about funerals. This will be a very muted affair as he had no close relatives, but –'

'I should like to come if you would like me to,' I broke in, and I heard him sigh.

'I should like it very much.'

'When is it?'

'Next Thursday at eleven. I'll pick you up soon after nine, if you really mean it.'

'Of course I do. I'll be ready.'

I put the telephone down. How nice not to hear about Henry Mawne. But how sad to think that I should not see that indomitable old man again.

As I undressed that night I thought of all the advice I had been given about my retirement.

All my friends had pointed out that I was bound to be lonely. I should wonder what to do with the empty hours before me. I should miss the hubbub of school life, the children, the companionship and so on.

In the diary, before coming upstairs, I had made a note of Uncle Sam's funeral and had observed that every day in that week, and the next, had some event to which I was committed.

Fat chance of being lonely, I thought a trifle bitterly. I had imagined myself drowsing on my new garden seat, and studying the birds and flowers around me in a blissful solitude. So far, that had been a forlorn hope. Far from being lonely I seem to have had a procession of visitors beating a path to my door like someone or other (Thoreau, was it?), who had the same trouble, and for some reason I connected with a mousetrap. I reminded myself to look up *mousetrap* in the *Oxford Book of Quotations* in the morning.

The telephone too was a mixed blessing. While it was a pleasure to hear one's friends, it always seemed to ring when one was getting down to the crossword. I recalled Amy's concern about my loneliness when I retired.

'Do *join* things,' she urged me. 'Go on nice outings with the National Trust. Caxley branch gets up some super trips, and you'd meet lots of like-minded people. And there are very good concerts and lectures at the Corn Exchange, and no end of coach parties going up to the Royal Academy exhibitions or the Barbican or the South Bank. There's no need to *vegetate*.'

Amy, and all the other well-intentioned friends, took it for granted that I should long for a plethora of people and excitements. As I climbed into bed I was reminded of a remark of Toddy's in *Helen's Babies*.

Does anyone these days read that remarkable book published at the turn of the century, decribing the traumas of a bachelor uncle left in charge of his two young nephews?

The conversation has turned to presents. Budge, the elder boy, wants everything from a goat-carriage to a catapult. Toddy, aged three, says he only wants a chocolate cigar.

'Nothing else?' asks his indulgent uncle. 'Why only a chocolate cigar?'

'Can't be bothered with lots of things,' is the sagacious reply.

I decide that I have a lot in common with Toddy, as I turn my face into the pillow.

The weather was as sad as the occasion when we set out on Thursday morning for the funeral. Rain lashed the car, the roads were awash, and every vehicle seemed to throw up a few yards of heavy spray. We spoke little on the journey. John was concentrating on his driving, and I was feeling tired and sad.

We drove straight to the church which was some half a mile from the nursing home. A verger in a black cassock showed us into a front pew. There were very few people in the other pews, but I noticed the matron of the nursing home and one or two elderly people with her, whom I guessed were friends and fellow-residents of Uncle Sam's.

His coffin lay in the aisle in the middle of the sparse congregation. It bore a simple cross of white lilies, no doubt, I thought, a tribute from the little gathering across the aisle.

It was bitterly cold, with that marrow-chilling dampness which is peculiar to old churches. I felt anxious for the old people nearby, and glad that I had put on a full-length winter coat.

The organ began to play, and the officiating priest entered with one attendant, and as we rose I noticed for the first time two magnificent flower arrangements flanking the altar. They were composed of yellow carnations shading from cream to deep bronze and formed a glowing background to the black robe of the clergyman.

The service was simple but moving. After the blessing we moved slowly outside, and talked in the shelter of the porch to the other mourners.

The rain still lashed across the countryside. The yew trees dripped, the grass in the churchyard was flattened in a cruel wind, and a vase of dahlias on one of the graves blew over, scattering vivid petals to the wind.

The undertakers had driven Uncle Sam's remains to the crematorium. Cars arrived to collect his old friends and return them to their luncheons, and John and I sought the shelter of his car.

'We need something to keep out the cold,' said John. 'Would you have any objection to eating at the place we did before, with Uncle Sam? It's nearby and we liked it, didn't we?'

I said it would be perfect, and we set off.

'Nice service,' I said. 'Cheerful, but dignified. And the flowers were lovely.'

'The nursing home did the lilies,' said John, 'so I plumped for the carnations for each side of the altar. They looked pretty good I thought.'

'Splendid,' I told him.

'Well, the old boy was a great carnation grower in his heyday, and always had some beauties in his greenhouse. "Must have one for my buttonhole each day," he used to say, "and some for a bouquet for any lady that takes my fancy."'

We had to run from the car into the shelter of the bar, where a log fire, a real one with flames, welcomed us.

'What's yours?' asked John, helping me off with my wet coat. 'And don't say orange juice! It's too dam' cold. Have something stronger today.'

And so I did.

We were due at the crematorium, for our final farewell to Sam, at two o'clock. There were even fewer people present, although the good matron was there with two or three of the hardiest residents, who must have forgone their afternoon rest to see the last of their old friend.

The service was conducted by the same young clergyman. I was much impressed by his beautiful voice and the kindness of his manner when talking to us after the ceremony.

'He'd make a splendid bishop later on,' I told John, as we drove home. 'I must make a note of his name, and look out for his progress in years to come.'

'Let's hope you're right,' said John, 'and by the way, I have news for you. I'm off to Portugal next week.'

'Lucky you! Or is it just business?'

'No, pleasure. Golf, in fact. I ran across an old school friend in town a month or two ago, and he and his brother own a villa out there.'

'It sounds marvellous.'

'They're both married with children, and they go out in turns during the school holidays. He reckons it works out quite cheaply, and they all love the country. What's more, there's a first-class golf-course nearby.'

'I didn't know you played.'

'I haven't for years, but I'm quite looking forward to it.'

'Is this villa in the Algarve?'

'No, somewhere on the west coast near Estoril. They let the villa when they're not using it, I gather. Quite a sound investment so far, Bill said.'

'It sounds so.'

By now we were close to Beech Green, and I invited John to tea. We were both tired, and I was still feeling cold. I asked John if he felt the same.

'Just a bit,' he admitted. 'Shall I light your fire?'

He got on with the job while I busied myself with the kettle and some cake.

'This is more like it,' said John when I had poured out, and the fire was burning nicely.

'A holiday will do you good,' I assured him. 'I felt fine after that week in Florence. You didn't say how long you would be away in this super villa.'

'Just the week, but I might think of taking it again if it's as splendid as Bill says.'

He looked at me speculatively.

'I thought perhaps it might be just the thing for our honeymoon one day.'

'Well, you think about it, John dear,' I said kindly, 'but count me out. More tea?'

5 The Invalid

As TIME passed, the pattern of my days fell into a pleasant order.

I still woke up about seven, but allowed myself the luxury of staying in bed a little longer than in my working days.

When teaching I had a rough and ready timetable of early morning routine, getting downstairs about twenty to eight, dressed for the day, and ready to feed Tibby inside and the birds outside, take in the milk, collect my school work together, eat my breakfast and clear it away, and then set off for Fairacre.

Nowadays I lingered over my toilet, Tibby's, the birds' and my breakfast, and relished the arrival of the post and paper, both of which had usually arrived, in my working days, after my departure.

I thoroughly enjoyed this easing of pressure, and when I thought of school it was usually with the happy feeling that I had no need to be there. But I still found myself looking at the clock and thinking: 'Now they should be doing arithmetic,' or 'I wonder if it's fine enough for the children to play outside at Fairacre?'

Sometimes too, on my walks, I would see something

interesting, a spray of blackberries, some hazelnuts or a particularly fascinating fungus, and would think how well it would look on the classroom nature table.

But these were only passing reminders of schooldays, and I was very content with my new and idler life.

About once a week I drove to Fairacre, chiefly to buy stamps and to purchase groceries from Mr Lamb's shop, as I had done for so many years. Always I returned with up-to-date gossip as well as my bag of groceries, so that I felt in touch with all the goings-on in Fairacre.

I was careful not to mention Henry Mawne's troubles, but Mr Lamb soon told me that Henry had gone to Ireland and no one knew when he proposed to be back.

A fresh piece of news was that Joe Coggs' mother had found a part-time job in Caxley, filling the shelves in one of the supermarkets. Mr Lamb hoped that the extra money would help to pay off some of the debts which were still outstanding at his own modest establishment.

After depositing my shopping in the car on this particular afternoon, I took a walk about the village I knew so well. There were signs of autumn everywhere. The horse-chestnut tree outside the Post Office was shedding green prickly fruits which split open on impact with the ground to disclose the glossy nuts within. Conker time was here again, and Jane Summers would have to cope with the clash of conker strings at playtime.

I went as far as the bend in the lane from which I could see Fairacre school, but went no further. It was very quiet. The children were probably listening to a story.

I did not propose to call. Once one has left a post, I think it wiser to stay away. Too often I have heard friends telling hor-

rific stories of former heads dropping in, far too frequently, to give advice or simply to see what is going on in their former domain. Nothing can be more annoying, and I intended to wait until invited to return to Fairacre school.

I liked Jane Summers. She had been to tea with me at Beech Green, and I had been invited to her house in Caxley. I suspected that I would be invited to Fairacre school's Christmas party with all the other friends of the school, and that would be an enormous pleasure.

Meanwhile, I stood and looked at the quiet little building which had been the hub of my life. As I watched, a little girl came out of the infants' room outer door, and dashed across the playground to the stone wall. Here she paused, unaware of my watching eyes, snatched a garment from the top and returned to the classroom, skipping cheerfully as she went.

I could imagine the preliminaries to this trip. Mrs Richards, probably reading a story, would see the upraised hand.

'What is it?'

'I bin and left my cardigan out the back.'

'Then go and fetch it. And be quick.'

And so the delighted escape into the playground, the retrieving of the garment, and the obedient return to the rest of the story, after the refreshing break.

It was a heartening glimpse. Obviously, things continued much as usual at Fairacre school.

Mrs Pringle told me more about the ongoing saga of Henry Mawne and his troubles.

'Do you know, he *flew* to Ireland? Costs a mint of money to fly there. Most people go on a boat, Ireland being an island. That's why it's called *Ireland*, I suppose.'

She paused, looking at me for confirmation. I felt unequal to making any explanation, and she continued her narrative.

'Alice Willet was up there when Mrs Mawne rang up. She was on that telephone for the best part of twenty minutes, and this at *midday*! No waiting for cheap-rate time. No wonder they're short of money.'

'I believe it's raining,' I said, looking out of the window.

Mrs Pringle brushed aside this pathetic attempt to change the subject, and she continued remorselessly.

'Give him his due he did pay Alice at the end of the morning, and told her not to bother to call until he sent word. He went off that afternoon to Bristol, I think it was.'

She picked up a saucepan from the draining board and scrutinized it closely.

'What's been in here?'

'Only milk.'

'I'd best give it a proper do. Have you had a go at it?'

'Yes. Just before you came. What's wrong with it?'

'It's dirty. Give you germane poisoning, as like as not.'

Mrs Pringle's use of 'germane' instead of, I imagine, 'ptomaine', so intrigued me that my annoyance vanished. So often she gets a word half right, which makes it all the more potent. For instance, I have heard her refer to the slight stroke I suffered as 'Miss Read's inability', instead of 'her disability'.

However, with her opinion of my capabilities, perhaps 'inability' is nearer the mark.

As I drove her home after her ministrations, she told me a little more about Mrs Coggs' new duties at the supermarket.

'She has to be there from four till seven, so Joe gets the meal.'

'Can't that wretched Arthur get the children's meal? Don't tell me he's in work.'

'No. He's inside again. Shoplifting this time. Fairacre's quite peaceful without him.'

'Do you mean that Joe actually cooks a meal, or does his mother leave things ready?'

I had visions of overturned boiling saucepans, frying-pans on fire, and the Coggs children being rushed to Caxley hospital.

'You know how they live,' said Mrs Pringle sourly. 'She leaves a loaf of bread out and the jam pot, and that's it. Though I did hear as Joe heated up a tin of soup for 'em one cold day. He forgot to turn off the gas, but luckily their neighbour looked in, so all was well.'

I did not find this very reassuring, and returned home after depositing my companion, with grave misgivings about the safety of the junior members of the Coggs family during their mother's working hours.

But what could I do about it? Mighty little, I told myself sadly, turning into my drive.

*

I spent that evening at Amy's. James was away and she asked me to keep her company.

We sat watching a very old film in what someone once called 'nostalgic black and white' and thoroughly enjoyed it.

'I wonder why,' commented Amy at one stage when the heroine was crying copiously, 'women in films never have a handkerchief and have to be given one by the leading man? I suppose the film-makers think it is touching, but does any woman go out without a handkerchief? I doubt it.'

'You told me once,' I reminded her, 'of two sisters who used to go out with one hanky between them, frequently asking: "Have you got *the handkerchief*?"'

'That's absolutely true,' Amy assured me. 'By the way, I heard from Lucy Colegate. She's got her sister staying with her. She's just lost her husband.'

'What, Lucy? She's always losing husbands.'

'Now, don't be catty, dear. I know you and Lucy don't see eye to eye, but I quite like her. And it's the sister who has lost the husband. Lucy says she's quite numb with grief.'

'Poor woman. It must be absolutely devastating to lose one's other half. Like having a leg off. An awful amputation.'

Amy nodded.

'I can't bear to think how I'd feel if James died. As you say, I suppose one would just feel half a person.'

'Only for a time surely,' I comforted her. It was unusual to see Amy in such a sad mood. Perhaps the black and white weepie we had been watching had something to do with it. In the garden too the rain was tossing the trees in a dismal fashion.

'Time the Great Healer, and all that?' queried Amy.

'That's right. After a bit you would be bound to start again, getting interested in all sorts of things, doing a bit of travelling, visiting friends. And so on,' I ended weakly.

'Maybe,' said Amy, not sounding very sure. 'I suppose one would just have to find comfort in Little Things, as the agony aunts tell us in the women's magazines.'

'Such as?'

'Well, one suggestion was that you should read all the old love letters. Personally, I can't imagine any more upsetting activity, but I suppose some women might be comforted.'

'Have you still got James' love letters?'

'No. I threw them away years ago. We were moving all over the place, and the less luggage one had the better.'

I felt that this was the robust response which one expected of Amy.

'I think Little Things like *no snoring*,' said Amy, becoming more animated, 'might be some comfort. And not having any shirts to iron. I must say that I should find that of considerable consolation in the midst of my sorrow.'

'You are a very flippant woman,' I said severely.

'And a hungry one,' said Amy rising. 'It's all this emotion. Come and have some supper in the kitchen.'

So we did.

John Jenkins had rung me before his departure to Portugal, and had also sent a pretty view of some gardens in Estoril with the sea in the background, of that peculiarly hard blue which all seaside postcards seem to show, whether of the Isle of Wight or Amalfi.

He was expected back on Saturday, and the final line of his postcard read:

'Will ring when I return. Love, John.'

The last two words, I felt sure, had been read with great

interest by the Beech Green postman, but I was not particularly perturbed.

I half expected a telephone call during Saturday evening, but guessed that his flight might have been held up. No doubt I should hear tomorrow, I thought, as I went to bed.

But Sunday brought no call, and I assumed that he had stayed on in Portugal. It did occur to me in the early evening that I might ring his home, but George and Isobel Annett called in after evensong, and I thought no more of the matter.

On Monday morning I needed extra milk, and walked along to the obliging Beech Green shop to buy a pint. There were several people there, including Jessie, surname unknown to me, who was John's domestic help.

'Poor Mr Jenkins,' she said to me, as I stood waiting to pay for my milk. 'Isn't it a shame?'

Of course, by this time I had John in a Portuguese hospital with multiple injuries, and unable to speak a word of the language. Alternatively, he could be in the wreckage of an aeroplane at sea, with the rest of his fellow passengers.

'The doctor's with him now,' continued Jessie, hoisting an enormous hold-all from the floor. 'I shall look in later on.'

'But what's the matter? What's happened?'

'He was ill on the flight and went straight to bed on Saturday night. Been there ever since.'

She staggered out with her burden, and I left soon after.

Within half an hour, I walked into John's house bearing a few things which I thought might be acceptable to an invalid.

The doctor had gone, and the place was very quiet. I called up the stairs.

'Come up,' said a weak voice.

He sat in bed looking thoroughly wretched, propped against

his pillows. I was secretly shocked at his appearance. His smile, however, was welcoming.

'I'm so sorry I didn't ring, but we were held up for hours at the airport. It was two o'clock in the morning when I crawled into this bed, and I've been here ever since.'

'What is it? Shouldn't you be in hospital?'

'I didn't ring the doctor until this morning. Can't worry the poor devil on a Sunday.'

I thought privately that this was being far too altruistic. If I had been as ill as John obviously was, I should have got the doctor whatever the day of the week. This patient was obviously of far nobler stuff than I was.

'What did he say it was?'

'Some bug which affects you rather like the malaria one. High temperature, shaking, nausea, all that.'

'When did it start? In Portugal?'

'I felt lousy on the plane. Some fly had bitten me earlier in the day, and it itched like mad. Doctor seems to think that started it. Anyway by the time I got home I was only fit for bed and quarts of water.'

'What can I do?'

'Nothing. Just stay and talk. Jessie is coming in every morning and evening, and she takes my sheets and pyjamas. I get soaked every few hours. With *sweat*, I hasten to add.'

I remembered Jessie's burden and felt guilty.

'I could wash some things for you.'

'I can't think what the neighbours would say if they saw my pyjamas blowing on your washing line.'

'To hell with the neighbours!'

John laughed. It was a wheezy laugh, and a weak one, but good to hear.

'That's my girl! But don't worry. Jessie's got a tumble drier, and she's taken everything at the moment.'

'Can I get you a drink?'

I made for a jug of orange juice standing nearby, but he grimaced.

'What I'd really like is a great mug of tea,' he said.

I went to get it, and when I returned he was lying back with his eyes shut. It was alarming, and he must have sensed my concern for he sat up again and spoke cheerfully.

'You could do something for me if you happen to be going to Caxley today.'

'I'm definitely going to Caxley today.'

'Well, could you get my prescription made up? And dare I ask you to buy me some more pyjamas? I'm running out of them pretty fast.'

'Of course. What size?'

He told me, and added:

'Three pairs, I should think. Any sort.'

I studied the pair he was wearing. They were the traditional blue and white striped things, probably made of winceyette. They reminded me of my father's night attire.

'Like those?'

'Not necessarily. Thinner, I think. I've got some polka-dot ones which Jessie's just taken away. It's a pity you didn't come when I was wearing them. I look like Noel Coward.'

'I'll take your word for it. I think I'd better get drip-dry ones to save Jessie some work.'

We sipped our tea in companionable silence for a few minutes. I felt very uneasy about him.

'Did the doctor mention hospital? I don't like the idea of you being alone. What about a nurse?'

'If you're offering, I can't think of anything nicer.'

'I'm the world's worst nurse,' I told him.

'This bug I've got gives you a pretty foul time for a week or two, but according to the quack it runs a predictable course and all one can do is to sweat it out and drink pints of liquid. The temperature drops after a bit, and apart from feeling like a wet rag one survives eventually.'

'But should you be alone? What about getting to the loo or having to fetch something from downstairs?'

'My dear love, and I mean that,' he said, suddenly earnest. 'I can get to the loo. I've even had a shower or two. I'm not eating, and the doc says that's OK as long as I *drink*. So I'm quite all right, and there's not a thing I need. Except your company, of course.'

I collected the mugs and stood looking at him.

'If Jessie's coming night and morning, I'll come and get your liquid lunch each day, and see what you need.'

He had a telephone by the bed, and I nodded to it.

'And *any* time, do ring. I'll come like a shot. You know that.'

'Suppose it is in the middle of the night? What would the neighbours say?' he laughed.

'You know what I think about the neighbours! Now I'm off to Caxley. Anything else you want?'

'You know what I want.'

I bent to give him a farewell kiss. His forehead was wet with sweat.

'You're terribly *dank*!'

'That's a fine thing to say to an invalid. You make me sound like a dungeon.'

'What you need,' I told him, 'is a few hours' sleep.'

'Maybe you're right.'

He was already slipping down the bed as I departed on my mission to Caxley.

*

I parked behind the same shop where I had recently bought tights and boxes of soap.

The men's department was virtually unknown to me, and seemed very quiet and austere compared with the toiletries and haberdashery departments I usually frequented.

There was only one other customer in there, a man absorbed in turning over piles of pants and discussing with the shop assistant the merits of various weights of garment.

An elderly man hurried to serve me. He had a pink and white face, white hair and moustache, and half-glasses. He reminded me of an old gentleman who used to keep our local sweet shop when I was a child.

I explained my needs, and he held before me an oblong package wrapped in shiny cellophane, just as the sweet-shop owner

66

had been wont to hold out a flat dish of Everton toffee, complete with a small hammer for breaking it up, so many years ago.

He slipped the contents out of the bag and displayed the pyjama jacket. It was of some satin-like crimson material with black frogging across it. It reminded me of the sort of costume a Ruritanian prince used to wear in musical comedies in the 1920s. I could not see John in this confection.

'I think something *quieter*,' I said. He turned to the shelves and added three more packets to the first.

These were certainly more normal, the sort of uninspired garment sported that morning by the invalid. They also looked as though they would take hours to dry, even in Jessie's tumble drier.

'Have you got any non-iron pyjamas?' I asked, turning over the heavy ones before me.

'Hello,' said someone beside me. It was my former assistant at Fairacre school, Mrs Richards.

'What are you doing playing truant on a Monday?' I said, secretly rather taken aback in the midst of my male shopping.

'Half term,' she said succinctly.

'Of course. My goodness, it'll soon be November.'

She was eyeing the pile of pyjamas with considerable interest. I supposed resignedly that news of my purchases would soon be known to Fairacre. Ah, well!

'Getting Christmas presents already?' she hazarded.

'That's right,' I lied.

'Now these,' said my assistant returning, 'are our usual nylon sort. We sell a lot of these, particularly for summer wear.'

I looked at them. They were cold and slippery. They looked as though they would be horribly chilly for a feverish body. Possibly *dank* too after an hour's wear, I decided.

'Well, I'll leave you to it,' said Mrs Richards. 'I'm looking for a larger belt for Wayne.'

'You feed him too well,' I responded, before turning back to my task.

'Or these,' added my nice old gentleman, drawing out some light-weight pyjamas in a rather nice grey and white Paisley pattern. They felt warm but thin.

'A very nice crêpe,' enthused the man. 'Just come in. Fully washable, drip-dry and thoroughly approved by the medical profession.'

That clinched it.

'I'll take three pairs,' I said, getting out my cheque book.

6   Back To School

THE PATIENT made steady progress. Jessie went in morning and evening, and I cooked his midday meal, such as it was. For the first few days he only wanted liquids, but quite soon came the great day when he clamoured for bacon and eggs.

He had lost weight and tired easily, but the fever had gone after a week or two, and the doctor pronounced him fit soon after that.

I ceased my regular midday ministrations when he insisted that he could cope again, and perhaps it was as well that I was able to do so, for I had a surprising telephone call from the local education office one foggy November morning.

'Miss Read?'

'Speaking.'

'Francis Hannen here.'

He was the local education officer, a cheerful fellow who had held the post for a couple of years now. What could he want?

'We wondered if you could help us out.'

'In what way?'

'Miss Summers has been smitten with the prevailing flu

bug, but it has given her acute laryngitis, and she is speechless.'

'Poor soul! What an affliction for a school mistress.'

'It is indeed. Well, we've rung one or two ex-teachers on our list, but they are either in the same boat, or away, and I hardly liked to bother you when you are so recently retired, but –'

His voice faded away.

'How long for?'

'The doctor insists on a week, maybe longer.'

I mentally checked my engagements for the week. It was Friday today. That would give me time over the weekend to collect my wits and a few teaching aids. John Jenkins was now able to cope without help from me, and only a shopping trip with Amy lay ahead on Tuesday.

'Of course I'll stand in.'

There was a gusty sigh.

'Marvellous! Miss Summers will be so relieved. Her sister is with her at the moment, so I'll ring and tell her straight away. A thousand thanks. I'm sure the children will be thrilled to have you back.'

I was not so sure about it, but with mutual well-wishing we rang off.

Over the weekend I did a certain amount of telephoning myself. First, of course, to Miss Summers' house where I had news of the invalid from her sister.

'She seems a little better. Temperature down a trifle, and the throat not so sore, but not a sound comes from her. The house is remarkably quiet, and I find myself whispering to Jane. It's quite uncanny.'

Then to Amy to postpone the shopping trip, and then to Mr Lamb at Fairacre asking him to pass a message to Mrs Pringle about her usual Wednesday visit.

That evening she rang me, obviously delighted to be among the first with my dramatic news.

'It'll be quite like old times,' she said with such gusto that it sounded welcoming. This was a pleasant surprise, until she added:

'I'll come a bit earlier each morning while you're at the school. There's always more to clear up.'

'Thank you, Mrs Pringle,' I replied, hoping it sounded as sarcastic as I meant it to be, but she was not abashed.

'And I'll be at your place as usual Wednesday afternoon, catching the Caxley.'

'The Caxley' in this instance meant the Caxley bus. Sometimes 'The Caxley' means the *Caxley Chronicle*, as in 'I read it in the *Caxley*, so I know it's true.' The local inhabitants of these parts are loyal readers.

I also rang John to tell him where I would be the following week. There was no need to of course, I told myself, but it seemed the civil thing to do after our extra close ties recently.

He sounded aggrieved.

'Surely you're not tying yourself up with *teaching*, all over again?' His voice was querulous. 'I hoped I could bob in now and again, now that I'm back on my feet.'

I bit back the sharp retort I should like to have made, and as I put down the receiver reminded myself that he was still convalescent.

Men, I thought disgustedly, are selfish to the core.

I set out on Monday morning with mixed feelings. Part of me welcomed this return to my old pastures, but I also felt remarkably nervous.

Several children were already running about in the playground, and they rushed to the car as I got out.

'You going to teach us again?'

'Just for a week,' I replied.

'Will Miss Summers be back then?'

'Is she really ill?'

'Is she in hospital?'

'She learns us lovely.'

'Lovelily,' I said automatically, lifting my case from the car. 'Beautifully, I mean.'

I was back sure enough.

The familiar school smell greeted me as I crossed the threshold, accompanied by my vociferous companions. It was a compound of coke fumes from the welcome tortoise stoves, disinfectant, which Mrs Pringle puts in the water to wash the lobby floor, and the general odour of an old building. It was wonderfully exhilarating, and I felt at home at once. I was surprised not to see Mrs Pringle, but a note on my desk explained all.

'Off to Caxley on the early bus. See you dinner time.'
   M. Pringle

Mrs Richards had not yet arrived. I banished the children to the playground, while I surveyed my old surroundings.

Basically, it was much as usual, but there were several innovations. For one thing, the ancient long desk that had stood at the side of the room for many years, had now gone. It had been a useful piece of furniture. The children put their lunch packets and fruit in season there, plums and apples from their gardens, or blackberries and hazelnuts collected on the way to school.

Toys, books and other treasures from home rested there, and at this time of year long strings of conkers festooned its battered top. I missed it. It was a relic of the past.

There was a very efficient-looking shelf of nature pamphlets which was new to me, and the framed pictures had been changed from such old friends as *The Light of the World* by Holman Hunt (so useful as a mirror with its dark background) and *The Angelus*, to modern prints of the French Impressionists. I had to admit that they added lightness and charm to the walls, and remembered that the office had urged us to take advantage of the service of supplying pictures which could be borrowed for a month or more.

I unlocked the desk and took out the register. Something seemed strange about the desk, and then I realized that the ancient Victorian inkstand with its two cut-glass ink-wells, one for blue ink and one for red, was no longer in place.

The heavy object, with its great curved brass handle, had vanished, and although I had never used the thing, relying, as no doubt Jane Summers did, on two fountain pens for the marking of the register, I felt a pang of loss.

At that moment Mrs Richards arrived and greeted me with a smacking kiss. Half a dozen children who had come in with her, despite my express order for them to stay outside, were entranced by this display of affection.

The great wall clock, mercifully still in its accustomed place, stood at ten to nine. Joseph Coggs burst into the room and stood transfixed. A slow smile spread across his gypsy face and he took a deep happy breath.

'Can I ring the bell?' he said, as he had said so often to me.

I nodded assent. School had begun.

By the time the dinner lady arrived bearing shepherd's pie and cabbage, with bright yellow trifle for pudding, I felt that I had been back for weeks.

The dinner lady was as welcoming as the children had been,

and even Mrs Pringle, when she arrived to wash up, managed a small smile.

'Got Fred in bed again,' she announced. 'Same old chest trouble, wheezing like a harmonium. I popped in to get his subscription made up at Boots.'

I expressed my sympathy with the invalid, and told her about Jane Summers' progress.

'Well, I only hope she don't try to get back too soon. Mind you, she's bound to be worried with someone else muddling along. She's very tidy herself. Everything in apple-pie order here *now*.'

I did not care for the emphasis on the last word, but said nothing.

'You looked in the map cupboard?' she enquired. 'It's a sight for sore eyes. All them maps tidied up neat and labelled, and none of that mess of raffia and old plimsolls as used to be there encouraging the mice.'

'Good!' I said briskly, and walked away before I received any more broadsides. Reluctantly Mrs Pringle returned to her labours, and I set about preparing for the afternoon's work.

Driving home soon after four o'clock, I was alarmed at the tiredness which overcame me. I put the car away and put on the kettle. I lit the fire, and was thankful to sit in my comfortable armchair a few minutes later and to sip my steaming tea.

I reviewed the day. It had been interesting to see the changes my successor had made. She was certainly efficient and up to date, and from the remarks of the children she was obviously well liked. I liked her myself, appreciating her brisk cheerfulness and energy. It seemed that even Mrs Pringle approved, and that certainly was something.

This glimpse into my old world had done a great deal to confirm that I had been right to go when I did. It was plain that I just did not have the physical strength needed for sustained and energetic teaching. And what about my mental attitude, I wondered? Was I really forward-looking? Did I relish going on refresher courses, studying new methods of teaching various subjects, or even attending local educational meetings? The honest answer was a resounding 'No', and had been for more years than I cared to contemplate.

Not that I had been completely inactive, I consoled myself, but I had to admit that I had never been thrilled with the idea of leaving my fireside on a bleak winter's evening to listen to someone telling me how to improve my methods of teaching reading, for instance. In most cases, I well remember, the advice was 'to let the child come to reading when ready' and 'to provide reading matter well within the child's comprehension.'

I could think of a number of erstwhile pupils who would *never* have been ready to come to reading without coercion on my part, and a great many more whose reading matter would have been only comics if left to their own devices. Years of teaching had shown me that for every child who takes to reading like a duck to water and needs no help at all, there are half a dozen or so who need sustained daily teaching in the art, and a very hard slog it is for teacher and pupil alike.

I had done my duty for all those years to the best of my ability, and with many failings, but the pupils now there were getting a better education than I had been able to give them in the year or two before I left. I went to wash my tea cup, full of goodwill to Jane Summers and her little flock.

The next day the vicar called at the school and took prayers. Afterwards he told the children how lucky they were to have me back with them. Especially, he added, as I had not been too well myself.

This, I knew, would be related by my pupils to their parents with dramatic effect, so that Fairacre would assume that I was at death's door, and in no shape to take over from Jane Summers, even temporarily. However, there was nothing I could do about it but smile at the kindly vicar, and thank him for coming.

The second day passed more easily than the first, and I had time to notice how well the new families had settled. A Housing Trust, of which Amy's husband James was one of the directors, now owned several new houses in Fairacre, and the children of primary school age were now pupils at Fairacre school. The coming of these children had solved a problem which had beset the village for some years.

As numbers fell it had looked as if the school would have to close. The village, and I in particular, owed a great deal to the

Trust and the families they sponsored. Fairacre school looked safe for years to come.

It was such a mild afternoon for November that I decided to take the children for a nature walk, and Mrs Richards joined us with the infants' class.

It was quite like old times tripping along the village street towards the downs. I was really indulging myself, for I had always enjoyed these excursions from the confines of the classroom, and it did one's heart good to see the boisterous spirits of the children as they relished their freedom in the bracing downland air.

Of course, there was not the same natural bounty to be had as a nature walk in the summer. Then we would return with such treasures as brier roses, honeysuckle or cranesbill. We might even find an empty nest whose function was now past, and convey its miracle of woven grass, moss and feathers to the nature table at school.

Nevertheless, there was still treasure to be found such as berries from the wayfaring-tree and hips and haws. Someone found a snail's shell, another found a flint broken in half so that a granular silicic deposit glittered in the light.

We toiled up the grassy slopes until we were high above the village. It was too wet to sit on the grass, but we stood for a few minutes to get our breath back, and to admire the view spread out below us.

There was not much activity to be seen in Fairacre. Washing was blowing in some gardens. Mr Roberts' Friesian cows made a moving pattern of black and white as they grazed, and a red tractor moved up and down a nearby field as bright as a ladybird.

We returned to the village carrying our gleanings. John Todd had discovered a Coca-Cola tin among the natural beauties, and was prevailed upon to deposit it in the bin provided outside the Post Office, which he did under protest. The rest of the garnering was displayed on the nature table, and very attractive it looked.

By common consent I read a story from *The Heroes* by Charles Kingsley, which Jane Summers, I was told, had just started with them, and all was delightfully peaceful.

I was conscious of more attention being given to the newly decorated nature table than Theseus's exploits, but who could blame them?

That afternoon I arrived home in much better shape. Downland air and exercise? Or simply getting back into my old groove? It was impossible to say.

On Wednesday afternoon I arrived home in time to share a pot of tea with Mrs Pringle before running her home. As always, the place was immaculate. Mrs Pringle was a first-class worker, and it was worth putting up with her tales of woe.

After getting up to date with the state of her ulcerated leg (no better, and the doctor worse than useless), we proceeded to the reaction of the inhabitants of Fairacre to my present duties at the school.

'Great shame about Miss Summers everyone agrees. She was getting them children on a real treat. *And* they had to behave!'

I agreed that all seemed to be going swimmingly.

'Mr Lamb reckons that she's as good as a headmaster. Keeps them down to work. None of this skiving off for so-called nature walks.'

I ignored this side-swipe by offering the plate of scones.

'Not for me. I'm losing weight.'

I looked at the clock, and Mrs Pringle took the hint, rising with much effort and going to fetch her coat.

'Well, at least it's only for a week we all tell each other. Can't do much harm in that time.'

On the way home, she changed the subject of my inadequacies to the troubles of her niece Minnie Pringle, who lived at nearby Springbourne with a most unsatisfactory husband, named Ern, and a gaggle of unkempt children.

'She's looking for another cleaning job. Ern's keeping her short of money.'

I was instantly on my guard. I have suffered from Minnie's domestic methods on several occasions.

'Why is Ern keeping her short?'

'Hard up, I suppose,' said Mrs Pringle. 'I told her flat that she's not to worry you. Lord knows there's enough to do in your place each week, but I can cope without her muddling about.'

'Thank you, Mrs Pringle,' I said humbly.

Bob Willet appeared one evening that week, bearing some fine eating apples.

'They're good keepers,' he assured me. 'Lovely flavour.'

I complimented him on such fine specimens, but he halted me in mid-flow of thanks and admiration.

'They're my neighbour's. New chap's just moved in. Nice enough, but don't know a thing about gardening. A townee, you see.'

'He'll learn, I expect.'

Bob looked gloomy, and puffed out his walrus moustache in a great sigh.

'I doubt it. Do you know he's bin and dug up a great patch by the back door for what he calls "a car-port". It was the only bit of ground there as grew a decent onion. Enough to break your heart. I told him so when the cement-mixer arrived. D'you know what he said?'

'What?'

'He said there was plenty of onions in the shops! The shops!' added Bob in disgust.

'He may learn.'

'Never! He just don't have no interest in living things. He drives up to London every day. I'm fair sorry for him really. I offered to prune his fruit trees when the time comes. He was polite, and all that, but it's plain he don't care a button for them fine old apples he's got there. Fred Pringle's granny used to get first prize at the Horticultural Show every year with them russets. Still, to speak fair, he did say he'd advise me about investing my money.'

Bob gave an ironic laugh.

'I told him there was not much hope of that. Funny thing is

though, I can't help liking the chap. He's so strange, you know. Like a foreigner.'

He departed soon after, leaving me to ponder on his words.

'Like a foreigner' Bob had said, and, of course, he was. Bob Willet was a countryman as had all his forbears been. If you plucked Bob from his green garden and dropped him in the arid wastes of a city he would wither as surely as a plant in the same circumstances.

I remember him once saying to me: 'When I gets twizzled up inside, I goes down to the vegetable plot and earths up the celery.'

It was this close affinity with the land that gave him his strength and sanity. That's what people missed in the vast urban places where most had to live and work.

It went against Bob's grain to see that cement laid over the best onion bed in Fairacre. It flew in the face of nature, and in his bones Bob rebelled.

Of course, even in my time things had changed in Fairacre and Beech Green. Almost every household now had a car, if not two. Ease of travel meant that the breadwinner could leave his renovated country cottage and take the nearby motorway to work, leaving the village practically deserted during the day.

When I first took up my headship at Fairacre school the village was an agricultural settlement, as it had been for centuries. The majority of the people worked for the three or four farmers and landowners as farm labourers, carters, ploughmen, shepherds and so on. There were still one or two farm horses in regular use.

Over the years farming had changed. A farmer with only

two or three men could cope with the work, thanks to modern machinery and the change in farming methods.

The cottages were bought by strangers and refurbished. These were the people who were commuters, arriving home too late, and probably too tired, to do much gardening or to take an interest in village affairs.

No wonder Bob Willet looked upon them as strangers. But how good to know that he 'couldn't help liking the chap!'

I was still thinking about the changes to village life as I chopped up Tibby's supper. Soon all the old people who remembered that way of life would be gone, and what a pity it was that so much valuable social history will have vanished.

Perhaps everyone should keep a diary, I thought, putting down the saucer, or even keep the monthly parish magazine for future generations to study.

I recalled the tales that Dolly Clare had told me about her way of life as a child in this very cottage that I had inherited. Tales of mammoth washdays, fetching water from the well, clear-starching and goffering irons. Stories about gleaning, grinding the corn, using flails to separate the chaff from the grain, about country remedies and the use of herbs. Why had I not written it all down?

Alice Willet, Bob and Mrs Pringle too often dropped a remark which gave a fascinating glimpse of life as it had been so recently, and which was now gone.

Perhaps I should start myself? Or better still, get a tape recorder and get Bob and the other old people to record their memories. Maybe I would start a diary of my own as well in the New Year. After all, what pleasure I had enjoyed from reading other people's diaries, Francis Kilvert's, for example, or dear Parson Woodforde whose diary lay on my bedside table and took me into rural Norfolk in the eighteenth century whenever I cared to accompany him.

Well, I must think about it, and also urge others to keep a diary. What success would I have in my encouragement of others, I wondered?

I recalled that I had once urged Bob to write down his memories, and his reply had been: 'I've no fist for writing. It's only the gentry as has the time and the learning to put pen to paper.'

Nevertheless, I could try again, and a tape recorder could be my ally.

Full of such plans for the future, I went early to bed and slept soundly.

7   Disturbances

I HAD KEPT in touch with Jane Summers throughout my time at school. Her sister had answered for the first few days, but on the Thursday Jane spoke herself.

She sounded hoarse, but very cheerful, and said that she had been pronounced fit for work on Monday. She was profuse in her thanks before we rang off.

I was mightily relieved to know that I should not be needed. It had been an interesting break, but I should be glad to return to my peaceful retirement.

But was it peaceful, I asked myself? I remembered the pipe-dreams I had indulged in when I said farewell to Fairacre, the leisurely walks, the lounging on my new seat in the garden, the settling down to read in the afternoon at a time when I should normally have been teaching. Somehow such bliss had been interrupted by events.

I pondered on the problems of John Jenkins and Henry Mawne which had arisen, and those presented by Mrs Pringle every Wednesday, and possibly Minnie Pringle in the future. I remembered George Annett's increasing pressure to help with church activities, and even dear old Amy's well-meant efforts to marry me off. It dawned on me suddenly that almost all my worries came from *people*. Left alone I should be much more content in my retirement.

I looked through the window at the November scene. A few chaffinches foraged below the bird table. Two rooks squabbled over a bread crust. Otherwise all was silent and peaceful.

The bare branches of the copper beech and lime trees dripped gently after the night's rain. The grey trunks, so reminiscent of an elephant's hide, were streaked with moisture. Nothing moved, nothing could be heard.

Here was peace indeed, I told myself. If only people would leave me quite alone to relish my solitude then I should certainly enjoy that peaceful retirement which so many kind souls had wished for me.

> *Where every prospect pleases*
> *And only man is vile.*

Whoever wrote that knew his onions, I thought, turning from the window.

*

On Friday I said farewell to Fairacre school with a light heart. The vicar had called first thing to take prayers as usual and to thank me for my efforts during the week. He was so genuinely sorry to see me go that I felt quite guilty.

'But you will come again?' he pleaded earnestly. 'Should anything like this crop up again, I mean?'

I pointed out that it was the office's decision, and that I had only been asked this time because the flu bug had cut down the number of local supply teachers.

'Of course, of course, I do realize that, but it is so pleasant to see you here when I call in. Will you be coming to the Christmas festivities?'

I said that I hoped to be invited, and he left slightly comforted.

The children were refreshingly off-hand about my departure, saying how nice it would be to see Miss Summers again, and go on with the story she was telling them 'out of her head' about a Roman soldier who used to live in a camp up on the downs.

This was the first I had heard of Jane Summers' imaginative skills and I was full of admiration for her, and very conscious of my own limitations.

I did my best by leaving the sweet-tin replenished to the top, and by leaving a handsome pink cyclamen for their head-mistress as a welcome-back present.

Driving home I felt that I had done my poor best for the week, but trusted that now I could resume my leisurely existence.

During the evening John Jenkins rang sounding his usual cheerful self.

'I've been given a brace of pheasants, just right for cooking. Come and help me eat one of them on Sunday.'

I said that I should be delighted, and was he roasting them?

'No, no,' he said, sounding rather pleased with himself. 'I'm cooking them in a casserole with apple. I warn you, it's the first time I've tried the recipe. Are you still on?'

I assured him that I was and promised to be there just after noon.

Obviously he was now back to normal, and relishing one of his favourite hobbies. He was an adventurous cook, and I admired his willingness to experiment. I was still thinking how good it would be to see him again, when someone knocked at the door, and on opening it, I was surprised to see George Annett.

'Hello! Do come in.'

'Mustn't stop. I'm supposed to be in Caxley.'

This was typical of George Annett. He never seemed to stay in one place for long, but flitted from here to there like a bird on the wing. A restless fellow, I had always thought, but on this occasion he actually sat down, and I took an armchair opposite him.

He began to rummage in a large envelope, and took out a small pamphlet.

'Now, this,' he said in a schoolmasterish way, 'is the pamphlet we leave in Beech Green church for visitors to peruse. They are supposed to buy it, but more often than not they simply walk around the church with it, noting the things mentioned, and then dump it back on the table. And pretty grubby some of these get, I can tell you.'

I agreed that such conduct was highly reprehensible, but wondered privately what I was being asked to do about it.

I soon learned.

'The thing is that this little history is now rather out of date, and I wondered if you could possibly find time to up-date it. Now you've retired, I mean. I expect you find time rather heavy on your hands and it's the sort of thing you'd do so well. Have a look anyway. For instance, some of the memorial tablets are not mentioned, and the new stained-glass window should have a note. I'd give you a hand of course, when I have a spare minute.'

He glanced at the clock, gave a cry, and leapt to his feet.

'Must fly. Shall I leave it on the table?'

Within two minutes he had gone.

Peace came surging back as I resumed my seat and had a preliminary look at the pamphlet. So this was the great work I was supposed to rejuvenate! Now I was retired, as George had said, with 'Time heavy on my hands' (a chance would be a fine thing!), here was something to console me.

I studied it more closely. Penned originally by a hand long dead, it was a dispiriting account of the church's attractions. The print was small, the paragraphs immensely long and the style pedantic. I wondered who could have been the author. I told myself that I must be particularly careful to keep my opinions to myself. It was bound to have been the work of some aunt, uncle or grandparent of a neighbour in Beech Green. No doubt any alteration of mine would be construed as vandalizing Holy Writ, but I agreed with George Annett that a new edition was needed.

The first thing to do, I decided, was to scrap the very poor photograph on the front. It must have been taken on a foggy day one winter's afternoon some fifty or more years ago, for it was indistinct and the trees, which now towered above the roof, were shown as mere saplings in the picture. Perhaps a nice bold wood-cut, or a really artistic modern photograph would liven things up?

At this juncture the telephone rang again, and it was Amy enquiring if I were still alive after a week's teaching.

'Just about,' I told her, and added that it had brought home to me the wisdom of retiring when I did.

She expressed her sympathy.

'What I really rang about was a recipe for gooseberry fool. Have you got such a thing? I seem to have half a dozen bottles of gooseberries in my store cupboard, and I thought I'd have a stab at gooseberry fool. The only thing is I believe you have to make a proper egg custard and I'm not sure if one uses the whites.'

'Don't burden yourself with egg-yolks, double saucepans and all that lark,' I told her. 'You'll have a sink full of dirty crocks and probably the custard won't have thickened. I'll post you my recipe unless you're coming over, but just use dear old Bird's custard and add plenty of cream.'

'Thanks for the tip,' said Amy. 'I'll pop over tomorrow evening if that suits you.'

'Perfectly.'

'And who were you buying three pairs of pyjamas for?'

'Never end your sentence with a preposition,' I countered, playing for time.

Now how on earth could Amy, at Bent, ten miles away, have heard of my purchases? I had half expected to have a comment or two from my Fairacre friends, but obviously Mrs Richards' momentary interest in the shop had passed, and she had made no comments. I was, as always, intrigued by this dissemination of knowledge.

'Don't be so pedantic,' said Amy. 'There's such a thing as common usage these days.'

'I bought them for John when he was ill,' I said. 'But how on earth did you know?'

'Charlie, who helps us in the garden when it suits him, was buying his winter pants at the same time.'

I remembered the only other customer in the men's department who had seemed totally absorbed in choosing his winter underwear. Ah well! That was explained.

'And how is John?' she went on.

'Fine now. He's giving me Sunday lunch. Pheasant cooked with apples.'

'Lovely!' enthused Amy, but whether she was so delighted at the thought of pheasant cooked with apples or my approaching visit to John Jenkins, was anyone's guess.

'See you tomorrow then,' she cried, and rang off.

Sunday dawned so bright and fair it might have been May rather than November. Only the bare trees outlined against a tender blue sky, and the shagginess of the lawn showed the true time of year. But the air was warm, the birds sang, and there was even a drowsy bumble-bee trying to get in at the window.

My spirits rose to match the sparkling day as, dressed in my best and bearing a pot of honey for my host's delectation, I set out for John's house.

The congregation of Beech Green church was just emerging from the porch. Someone raised a hand to me, and I tooted the horn in reply, edging out to turn away from all these good folk as I went towards my old parish.

I wondered why I felt so remarkably buoyant. Was it just the weather? Was I feeling devil-may-care because I had skipped church that morning? Was it because I knew that my new suit was unusually becoming? Or was it, I wondered with some misgiving, that I was going to see John Jenkins?

I hoped it was not this last reason. Much as I enjoyed John's

company I had no intention of accepting him as a suitor although he had offered marriage often enough, heaven alone knew. I had lost count of the times he had proposed and been kindly, I hoped, rejected by me. No, I decided, turning into John's drive, it was just a happy amalgamation of all those factors that contributed to my well-being. I should continue to enjoy that happy state.

The most delicious aroma was wafting from John's kitchen, the honey was warmly received, and within five minutes we were sipping sherry in John's sunlit sitting room.

He was looking remarkably fit, and confirmed that he had now completely recovered from what he described as 'the Portuguese Peril'.

'And what have you been up to, besides deserting me for Fairacre school?'

I told him about George Annett's church pamphlet, and he was all in favour of a new edition.

'Nothing more off-putting than a dreary photo and small print,' he agreed. 'An aunt of mine tried to get me interested in *Lorna Doone* when I was about ten, and gave me a horrible edition with those shiny sepia pictures which look as though they have been executed in weak cocoa. It put me off for life.'

'Like double columns down the page,' I added, 'beloved of Victorian editors.'

'I'd better prod the bird,' said John, making for the kitchen. 'Come and give me your advice.'

I followed him to the oven and watched him raise the casserole lid. Everything smelt wonderful, but we agreed that the lid should now be removed so that the bird could brown.

We returned to our sherry and the conversation turned to the subject of recording the memories of the older generation.

'And ourselves,' added John. 'We're knocking on, and I don't suppose there are many of us left who can remember the Schneider Trophy air race, or even the Abdication.'

'That was quite something,' I agreed. 'The children used to sing: "*Hark the herald angels sing, Mrs Simpson's pinched our King*".'

'I like that,' said John delighted. 'I was in Kenya then, and feelings ran high.'

He put down his glass.

'Which reminds me,' he went on, 'if you really want to go on with this recording business, I have a tape recorder I can lend you. I bought it when I came back from Kenya. Do borrow it.'

I expressed my thanks, but wondered if I should ever get down to embarking on this worthy project.

'Perhaps keeping a diary would help,' I pondered. 'But I suppose it would be best to start that next January.'

'It sounds to me,' said John firmly, 'as if you are pro-crastinating. My father's motto was: "Do it now", which I found a little daunting at the time, but I can see the point now.'

'I suppose I'm beginning to get a reaction from my week's teaching,' I said. 'I have a feeling that my life might get a bit aimless.'

'Make me your aim,' suggested John. 'Think how rich and full your life would be married to me.'

'Is that today's proposal?'

'Of course. Or would you prefer a more passionate one after the pheasant?'

'I reckon that pheasant will be done,' I replied. 'Shall we investigate?'

It was, and very soon we settled down to enjoy the tasty meat. The fluffy apple in which the bird had been resting was deliciously flavoured with its juices and with the red wine which had been added. John had also cooked pears in red wine, explaining that as he had opened a bottle of good claret to moisten the pheasant dish, he felt it should be used up.

I complimented him on such exemplary domestic economy. He certainly was a very capable man, I thought, watching him prepare coffee. Really, one could quite see his attractions as a husband. But not for me, of course.

It was while we were enjoying our coffee that the telephone rang. Whoever it was at the other end must have been in full spate, for John's answers were sparse.

'No bother at all,' he said at last. 'I'll be there at three, without fail. See you then.'

'Henry,' he said. 'Ringing up from Ireland. I'm picking him up on Wednesday at Bristol airport.'

'With Deidre?'

'He didn't say. He sounded rather flustered, and kept

apologizing. I don't know why. I told him I'd meet him if he decided to come home at any time.'

'I do hope they've made it up. Poor old Henry is a bit lost on his own.'

'Well, don't take pity on him if he is. It's his own fault. There are far more deserving cases of lone men nearer home, you know. Would you like to hear more about one of them, or have a walk round the garden?'

'I think,' I said, putting down my empty coffee cup, 'I could do with a walk round the garden after that delicious meal.'

'Ah well!' said John, rising. 'There'll be another time, no doubt.'

'I was afraid of that,' I told him, laughing.

I drove home from John's feeling remarkably well in body, but disturbed in spirit. There was really no reason, I told myself, why I should concern myself about Henry Mawne. He and Deidre were quite old and experienced enough to know what they were doing, so why should I bother?

To be honest, I knew the answer. I just did not want the added complication of Henry's intrusion into my own life. Over the years he had caused me embarrassment and annoyance, and now with John to further complicate matters, I just prayed that Deidre would be accompanying her husband back to a settled life in Fairacre.

Another thought was niggling too. John's offer of his tape recorder had brought to the fore this nebulous idea of writing a book, or booklet, or perhaps a series of articles for the *Caxley Chronicle* based on the recordings I might be successful in wheedling from my older friends.

I had told John that I had felt somewhat restless after my week's work at Fairacre. This was true, but was it only transient? Did I really want to work again? I certainly did not intend to give up the delight of staying day-long in my own beloved cottage, and going out to some place of business.

Perhaps this little job of George Annett's would help me to settle things? It would be a feeler, keep me busy and interested, and it would not be too demanding mentally. After all, I had appeared several times in the columns of our local paper. I had a slight but happy relationship with the present editor, and felt sure that he would take any of the local memories I was envisaging for future subject matter. Of course, if I really got a lot of material I might make a whole book and post the typescripts to the Oxford University Press or any other respected publisher.

Yes, I told myself, as I swung into my drive, the little pamphlet's up-dating should give me some idea of what I really wanted to do in retirement. I felt rather more settled in my mind as I unlocked the door and made my way into the sitting-room.

Here chaos confronted me. A starling had fallen down the chimney, and now dashed itself dementedly against the window-pane. I let it out and surveyed the wreckage.

The hearth was thick with soot. The carpet had a good sprinkling too, and my newly laundered loose covers on the sofa and chairs bore black claw marks and a light film of soot.

I went upstairs to take off my finery donned for the lunch party, enveloped myself in an overall, and went to fetch the vacuum cleaner, dustpan and brush, and a bucket of hot water and scrubbing brush.

The problems of future authorship, and those pertaining to Henry Mawne's troubles, were shelved.

I had enough of my own.

8   Christmas

PREDICTABLY ENOUGH November slipped quietly into December, and I had my annual shock on visiting Caxley to find that the shop windows were bedizened with Christmas trappings, and that there were men on tall ladders and a sort of fork-lift affair getting ready to string Christmas decorations across the High Street.

This year in particular I seemed to be unprepared. The fact that I had sent my overseas gifts off in good time had engendered a smugness which had insulated me against the stark truth that the bulk of my shopping had yet to be done.

An added factor was that for the first time I had had no Christmas preparations in school to keep me on my toes.

There was no time on that day to start Christmas shopping, and in any case I had not yet made a list of recipients and the right presents for them. I comforted myself with the thought that I had at least got all my cards in the cupboard upstairs, thanks to the RNLI and RSPB catalogues which had arrived on a scorching July day.

No doubt even that forethought would not be completely successful when the time came to write the cards. Usually, I had to scurry to Mr Lamb in Fairacre shop for a further dozen

of rather less superior articles. Any of my friends with sur-
names beginning with W, Y or Z were doomed to have cards
with lots of sparkle on them and unnecessary couplets of
doggerel inside.

It was Mr Lamb who first told me the news about Henry
Mawne. He had arrived home without his wife, and had said
little about her.

'There's talk of him selling the house,' said Mr Lamb,
adding two tins of Pussi-luv to the little heap of my purchases
on the counter.

'Oh, I hope he won't,' I cried. 'It's been in his family for so
long. I remember his aunt, Miss Parr, telling me about it.'

'Costs a mint of money to keep up, a place like that. They
say he might get something smaller in Ireland. Mind you, it's
not a good time to sell. No money about, and who wants a
great barn of a place like that?'

'Quite. I'm thankful I've only got a small cottage.'

'And a very nice one.' He looked at me speculatively.

'Now if you ever felt like selling,' he went on, 'I reckon
you'd soon find a buyer. I'd be interested myself, by the way, if
you ever decided to go into one of these flats attached to a
nursing home, for your last days as it were. I'm beginning to
think of retiring myself sometime. The shop's a great tie, and
the paperwork's something vicious.'

I was too stunned to reply, but paid my dues and left.

A short visit to Fairacre shop usually gave me food for
thought. I had plenty to mull over this time.

Did I really look so decrepit that my only option was a nursing home? Had I ever been foolish enough to say that I might
leave my cottage? I searched my mind, but had no recollection
of such a thing. In fact, I had always maintained that nothing
would induce me to leave Beech Green.

No, Mr Lamb, with his own retirement in mind, was simply putting out feelers, I told myself. But how aggravating it was, and what a cheek on his part!

My indignation continued for the time it took me to get home, and it was not until some time later that Henry Mawne's affairs crossed my mind.

Was there any truth in these rumours that his house might be for sale? Was he really contemplating going to Ireland? If so, did it mean that he was going to return to Deidre?

In any case, how did it affect me? To be honest, it would be a relief to have Henry Mawne out of my life. That was the over-riding fact, sad though I should be to see his fine old house in someone else's hands.

I began to feel a little sorry for him. Poor old man, he was getting on, and there seemed to be a lot of trouble ahead for him, one way or another.

Perhaps it would be simpler for him to give up his home and his wayward wife and just go into one of those nice flats attached to a nursing home, as recommended by Mr Lamb?

Who knows? I might meet him again there one day. It would be just like the gods to have the last laugh.

A day or two later, I found an invitation to a Christmas party at Fairacre school lying on the mat when I returned from a walk.

Jane Summers had probably dropped it through the letter-box on her way home to Caxley. I was sorry to have missed her, but was glad to see that she was prudently saving postage.

The invitation was written in a child's handwriting, and I put it in pride of place on the mantelpiece. That was one festivity I should look forward to attending.

Meanwhile I started to work on the church pamphlet. Basically, I decided, it provided useful facts about the building, but needed a few additions. For instance, a rather attractive stained-glass window in memory of twin sons killed in the First World War had no mention at all, which seemed a pity. The family was an ancient and honourable one whose seat had been at Beech Green for centuries. The last of the family had left in the fifties, and it was now a nursing home. (Perhaps it was this one Mr Lamb had in mind for me?)

There was also a fine Elizabethan tomb in the Lady Chapel, with rows of little kneeling children mourning their recumbent parents. This had been dismissed in the present leaflet with: 'The Motcombe tomb is to be found in the Lady Chapel.' I decided to give it more prominence in my version.

To this end I spent a happy morning in Caxley Library looking up the history of both families, and was surprised at how quickly the time passed whilst engaged on my simple researches.

Driving home I began to wonder if this sort of gentle activity was what I needed to fill my days in the future. I began to wax quite enthusiastic and wondered if a small book about local history would prove a worthwhile project. It could have maps in it, I thought delightedly. I like maps, and I imagined myself poring over old maps and new ones, and deciding how large an area I would cover, and what scale I should choose for reproducing them.

Caxley itself could provide a wealth of material for a volume of local history, but I decided that other people had done this before me, and in any case I had no intention of burdening myself with trips to the crowded streets of our market town to check facts and figures.

No, I shall concentrate on something simpler, Beech Green, say, or Fairacre. I remembered some of dear Miss Clare's memories of her thatcher father and his work, and of the way of life she had known as a child in the house which was now mine. If only I had written them down at the time!

Such pleasurable musings accompanied me as I went about my daily affairs. When at last I settled down one wet afternoon to write up my notes about the two families commemorated in my parish church, I began to have second thoughts.

This writing business was no joke. Both accounts were much too long. I did some serious cutting and editing, then began to wonder if my predecessor had discovered the same difficulty in describing the earlier tomb, which accounted for his terse advice to visit the Lady Chapel.

I put down my pen and went to make a pot of tea. I needed refreshment. Perhaps it would be better to devote my energies to recording people's memories, as I had first thought, and writing my own diary next year. I was beginning to realize that historical research and, worse still, writing up the results was uncommonly exhausting.

I had a chance to broach the subject of recording memories when Bob Willet arrived with Joe Coggs the next Saturday.

'We've come to split you up,' announced Bob.

I was not as alarmed as one might imagine. Translated it meant that he and Joe were about to divide some hefty clumps of perennials which had been worrying Bob for some time.

They went down the garden bearing forks and chatting cheerfully, while I went indoors to make some telephone calls.

I could hear them at their task. Bob was busy instructing his young assistant on the correct way to divide plants.

'You puts 'em back to back, boy. Back to back. Them forks.

Pretty deep. Put your foot on 'em, so's they gets well down. That's it. Now give 'em a heave like.'

I could hear the clinking of metal as the operation got under way, then a yell.

'Well, get your ruddy foot out o' the way, boy! You wants to watch out with tools.'

I hoped I should not be called upon to rush someone to hospital, and was relieved to hear no more yells, just Bob's homely burr as he continued his lesson.

Some time later, their labours over, we all sat down at the kitchen table with mugs of tea before us, and a fruit cake bought from the WI stall in the middle.

My two visitors did justice to it and Bob congratulated me.

'You always was a good hand at cake-making. My Alice said so.'

This was high praise indeed as Mrs Willet is a renowned cook. However, common honesty made me confess that I had not made this particular specimen.

I broached the subject of Bob's early memories, and drew some response.

'Well now, I don't really hold with raking up old times, but there's a lot I could tell you about Maud Pringle in her young days as'd make you sit up.'

The dangers of libel suddenly flashed before me. Perhaps old memories were not going to be as fragrant and rosy as I imagined.

'I wasn't thinking of *people* so much,' I began carefully, 'as different ways of farming, perhaps, or household methods which have changed.'

Bob looked happier.

'You can't do better than to talk to Alice. She remembers clear-starching and goffering irons and all that sort of laundry lark. She sometimes did a bit for old Miss Parr. She had white cambric knickers with hand-made crochet round the legs. They took a bit of laundering, I gather.'

I said I should love to hear Alice's reminiscences, and meant it.

'I could put you wise to old poaching methods,' said Bob meditatively. 'Josh Pringle, over at Springbourne, he was the real top-notcher at poaching. He'd be a help too, but I think he's in quod at the moment. He's as bad as our . . .'

Here he broke off, having recalled that young Joe was the son of the malefactor he had been about to mention.

'As I was saying,' he amended with a cough, 'Josh is as bad as the rest of them, but he'd remember a lot about poaching times, and dodging the police.'

I began to wonder if I had better abandon my plans for

enlightening future generations. Danger seemed to loom everywhere.

'Then there was that chap that worked for Mr Roberts' old dad,' went on Bob, now warming to the subject. 'Can't recall his name, but Alice'd know.'

'What about him?'

'He hung himself in the big barn.'

This did not seem to me to be a very fruitful subject for my project. Dramatic, no doubt, but too abrupt an ending.

'What about the clothes you wore as a child? Or the games you played?' I said, trying to steer the conversation in the right direction.

'Ah! You'd have to ask my Alice about that,' said Bob rising.

I said I would.

When they had departed, Bob with a message to Alice to ask if I might call to have a word with her about my literary hopes and Joe with the remains of the WI cake, I decided to ring John Jenkins.

I told him about my conversation with Bob Willet and my plan to visit Alice. Would it be convenient to borrow the tape recorder after I had seen her?

'Have it now,' urged John. 'I never use the thing, and if you've got it handy you may get on with the job.'

It sounded as though he doubted my ability to go ahead with the project.

'I'll bring it over straight away,' he said briskly, 'and show you how it works.'

He was with me in twenty minutes. I was relieved to see that the equipment was reassuringly simple, just a small oblong box which, I hoped, even I could manage.

'I think this plan of yours is ideal,' he said when he saw that I had mastered the intricacies of switching on and off. 'It's the sort of thing you can do in your own time, and there must be masses of material.'

'If it's suitable,' I commented, and told him about Bob Willet's memories of Mrs Pringle's youthful escapades and Josh Pringle's brushes with the law. He was much amused.

'Yes, I can see that a certain amount of editing will be necessary.'

He was silent for a moment and then added: 'You could tackle another local subject, I suppose. I mean some historical event like the Civil War. There were a couple of splendid battles around Caxley, and one of the Beech Green families played a distinguished part.'

This I knew from the church pamphlet I was altering, but I expressed my doubts about my ability to do justice to such a theme.

'I never know,' I mused, 'which side I should have supported.'

'As Sellar and Yeatman said in *1066 and All That*, the Royalists were Wrong but Wromantic, and the Cromwellians were Right but Repulsive.'

'Exactly. On the whole I think I'd have been a Royalist. Their hats were prettier.'

'So it's no-go with a historical dissertation?'

'Definitely not. I'll try my more modest efforts.'

I looked at the clock.

'Heavens! It's half past seven. You must be hungry.'

I mentally reviewed the state of my larder. A well-run pantry should surely have a joint of cold gammon ready for such emergencies. Mine did not.

'I could give you scrambled eggs,' I ventured.

'My favourite dish,' John said gallantly. 'You do the eggs and I'll do the toast.'

And so we ended the evening at the kitchen table, and were very merry.

The next time I saw Bob Willet he brought a message from his wife.

'Alice says could you put off this interview lark until after Christmas? What with the shopping and all the parties she's helping at, she can't see her way clear to think about old times.'

I said I quite understood and I would try my luck in the New Year.

In a way I was relieved. I too had a good many things to do before Christmas, and it would give me time to collect my thoughts about the proposed work.

'You're putting it off,' said Amy accusingly, when I told her.

'I know that, but the world seems to have managed without my literary efforts so far, and I reckon another few months won't make much difference.'

Meanwhile, much relieved, I finished my Christmas cards, decorated a Christmas tree for the window-sill, and looked forward to the party at Fairacre school.

Fog descended overnight, and the last day of term when the party was to take place, was so shrouded in impenetrable veils of mist that it seemed unlikely to clear.

Everything was uncannily still. Not a breath of wind stirred the branches or rustled the dead leaves which still spangled the flower beds.

There were no birds to be seen, and no sound of animal life anywhere.

There was something eerie about this grey silent world. One

could easily imagine the fears that plagued travellers abroad in such weather. It was not only the fear of evil-doers, the robbers, the men who snatched bodies from graves, the boys who picked pockets, but the feeling of something mysterious and all-pervading which made a man quake.

By midday, however, the fog had lifted slightly. It was possible to see my garden gate and the trees dimly across the road. No sun penetrated the gloom, but at least the drive to Fairacre would not be hazardous.

I wore my new suit and set off happily. This would be my first Christmas party as a visitor, and I looked forward to seeing all my Fairacre friends.

I was not disappointed. There were the Willets, the Lambs, Mrs Pringle with her husband Fred in tow, and of course the vicar and Mrs Partridge and a host of others.

Jane Summers, resplendent in a scarlet two-piece, and Mrs Richards in an elegant navy blue frock greeted us warmly, and I had a chance to admire the look of my old quarters in their festive adornment.

I was glad to see that the infants' end of the building still had paper chains stretched across it. The partition between the two classrooms had been pushed back to throw the two into one, and Miss Summers' end was decorated in a much more artistic way than ever it was in my time.

Here were no paper chains, but lovely garlands of fresh evergreen, cypress, ivy and holly. The splendid Christmas tree was glittering with hand-made decorations in silver and gold, and the traditional pile of presents wrapped in pink for girls, and blue for boys lay at its base.

I was pleased too to see that Mrs Willet had made yet another of her mammoth Christmas cakes, exquisitely iced and decorated with candles.

The vicar gave his usual kindly speech of welcome, and we were all very polite at first, but gradually the noise grew as tea was enjoyed. We were waited on, as usual, by the children and it was good to see how happy and healthy they looked.

The hubbub grew as we all moved about after tea, greeting friends and catching up with all the news.

'Mr Mawne hasn't turned up,' I heard Mrs Pringle say. 'But then I suppose he's got enough to think about.'

This was intriguing, but I was busy talking to Mr Roberts, the local farmer, and heard no more.

I had not noticed Henry's absence, but now I came to think of it, it was strange that he had not appeared. As a good friend of Fairacre school he had always been invited, and I felt sure that Jane Summers would have made a point of sending him an invitation. Perhaps he had another engagement, or was not well, or had returned again to Ireland? Who could tell? In any case, it was none of my business, I told myself.

People began to move off. The fog was thickening, and it was plain that we should have another black night.

I was sorry to leave my old haunts, and said goodbye to my successor and Mrs Richards with real regret. It was sad to leave the Christmas warmth and splendour for the cold murkiness outside, but I drove slowly home through the treacherous fog glowing with the aftermath of good food and good company.

Two days later, I set off for Dorset to spend Christmas with my cousin Ruth. I stayed with her until New Year's Day and returned wondering if I should be strong-minded enough to make the first entry in my new diary, as I had planned to do.

Years before, Amy had presented me with a large diary, and I had done my best to put a few meagre jottings into it through the months.

This time my new diary was a present from John, who was obviously going to see that I kept my nose to the grindstone.

I had every intention of doing my best. Over the years I have had so much pleasure from other people's diaries and I was interested to read recently that some psychiatrists recommend the activity. The theory, so I gathered, was that everyone needed 'a speech friend' with whom the small details of everyday living could be discussed. I promised myself that this diary would be my 'speech friend', and just as the great diarists of the past, Kilvert, Woodforde, Evelyn and Pepys, had put down their thoughts, so would I, in my small corner at Beech Green.

I recalled Virginia Woolf's comment on Parson Woodforde's diary-keeping: 'Perhaps it was the desire for intimacy.

When James Woodforde opened one of his neat manuscript books he entered into conversation with a second James Woodforde. The two friends said much that all the world might hear, but they had a few secrets which they shared with each other only.'

Even in the eighteenth century, it seemed, a 'speech friend' was a comfort. I too knew what it was to guard my tongue in a small community. In my diary I could relax and chatter away without any restraint or fear of gossiping tongues.

The day after my return, I took out John's handsome present, and with some excitement, laced with some trepidation, I made my first entry.

How long, I wondered, would I keep it up? Time alone would tell.

9 Problems Old and New

ONE BLEAK Wednesday afternoon in January Mrs Pringle arrived with news of Henry Mawne. I confess that I was eager to hear it, for I had not seen him for weeks, and the rumours about him were many and various.

The vicar, who had called to see me soon after Christmas, was sad and bewildered by Henry's circumstances, but seemed to know nothing of his plans.

Mr Lamb at Fairacre shop, my most reliable informant, was equally reticent.

'Well, I suppose you've heard about Mr Mawne,' began Mrs Pringle, as she hung up her coat and donned a cretonne overall.

'Not a word,' I told her.

'That's a surprise. I said to Bob Willet that if you didn't know then nobody did.'

I found this assumption that Henry Mawne would confide in me distinctly annoying, but said nothing.

'My cousin in Caxley said the house was going up for sale. It'll be in the *Caxley* this week.'

'But if it hasn't been advertised yet, how does your cousin know?'

'She works at the estate agent's office,' replied Mrs Pringle. I decided not to pursue that aspect of the news.

'I'm sorry to hear it. Henry will miss the place, I'm sure, and he has done marvels with the garden.'

'Well, he'll have to try his hand at gardening in Ireland, so I hear. They say he's going to get that new wife of his to see reason.'

I was unusually disturbed by this news, but tried to hide my feelings.

'Must be upsetting for you,' observed Mrs Pringle, eyeing me shrewdly. 'You and him have been through a lot together over the years. Want the windows done upstairs? I thought they were a disgrace last week.'

I gave my assent to the cleaning of the disgraceful upstairs windows, and went into the kitchen to ponder on this news.

It was maddening, of course, to have Mrs Pringle pitying me for what she enjoyed thinking of as my broken heart. My chief feeling towards Henry was irritation, and always had been. Nevertheless, he had many good points, and was an old friend. I was going to miss him.

But my chief concern was for Henry himself. His house and garden had always been dear to him, and to part with it now would be a terrible blow. Was it wise to throw away the pleasant life he had made for himself in Fairacre, to pursue an unpredictable future and a stormy marriage overseas?

I hoped he had found someone to advise him. No doubt his solicitor would have pointed out the pros and cons, and he must have many old friends with whom he could discuss his problems. I sincerely hoped that these troubles would soon be resolved for him, and that whatever the future held it would be happy.

Poor old Henry, I thought sadly! Well, at least he was

worrying this out on his own, as far as one could see. In the old days he had often brought his troubles to me, and I could not help feeling relieved that it seemed I was to be spared from any involvement in his present worries.

I should have known better.

Over our cups of tea, Mrs Pringle broached the subject of my work on old memories.

'I hear as you're having Alice Willet recorded,' she said, with some hauteur. 'Is it for the BBC?'

'Good lord, no!' I began to explain my modest aims, but she still looked offended. Could she be jealous of a tape recorder?

'I hoped you might tell me about some of your early memories too,' I said, doing my best to placate the lady. 'It needn't be recorded, of course. I could just make a few notes if you'd prefer it.'

'If Alice Willet's going to speak into one of those contraptions then I will too,' she said. 'I reckon my memory's as good as hers any day.'

'That would be fine by me,' I said hastily. 'I'd better see Alice first as I've mentioned it to her, and then I should love to hear your reminiscences.'

She looked somewhat mollified, accepted a piece of shortbread graciously, and things were back to normal.

As I drove her back to Fairacre, Mrs Pringle dropped her second bombshell.

'It's about Minnie,' she began, as the village came in sight.

'You know I don't want her to work for me,' I said firmly.

'I know that. And I don't want her messing up the work I do for you, I can assure you. It's quite bad enough getting your place clean without Minnie under my feet.'

My relief was short-lived.

'No, it was about something quite different.'

'What?'

'Bert.'

'Bert?' I squeaked in horror. 'What on earth is Bert to me?'

Bert is the most persistent of Minnie's admirers and the subject of many domestic rows in Minnie's home. Ern, her husband, is understandably jealous of Bert, and the police have often been called to break up a fight between the two men.

'Minnie wondered,' said Mrs Pringle, as I stopped at her gate, 'if you'd have a word with Bert and tell him to stop worrying her.'

'But, Mrs Pringle,' I expostulated, 'why me? I am certainly not going to do anything of the sort. Minnie's affairs are her own, and if she can't choke off Bert, with Ern's help, then she must call the police.'

'Ah well!' sighed Mrs Pringle, collecting her belongings. 'I told Minnie you'd say no, but she's got such an opinion of you. She says you could frighten Bert off with just one of your looks, but I told her how it would be. Still, I kept my word. I did mention it, didn't I, like I promised Minnie?'

'You did indeed,' I said, still seething. 'And now you must tell her that I absolutely refuse to have anything to do with the matter.'

Driving back I pondered on Minnie's touching faith in my disciplinary powers. Did I really have such a basilisk glare? It would have been nice to think I had, but it had certainly never worked on Mrs Pringle herself.

Galvanized into action by Mrs Pringle's remarks about Alice Willet's recorded efforts, I got in touch with my first contributor and arranged to bring to bring my tape recorder to her home one afternoon in the next week.

Making a date to suit us both was far from easy. Alice said that Monday afternoon was devoted to ironing, Tuesday was her Bright Hour afternoon, Wednesday she had to go to Springbourne manor house to shorten some curtains, Thursday, of course, was always out as it is Caxley market day, and would Friday be any good?

As Friday afternoon was the only day of that week when I too was engaged, we embarked on a long and complicated discussion about my calling on her after depositing Mrs Pringle on the Wednesday.

'Well, I think it could be done,' she said doubtfully. 'I'll be back from Springbourne by four, and Bob can have cold pilchards for his tea when he gets in.'

We left it at that, and I wondered how high-powered business men worked out their arrangements with clients abroad and their overseas flights, when Mrs Willet and I had such difficulty in finding an hour together in our comparatively tranquil lives.

But was it tranquil? I still wondered about that peaceful retirement I was supposed to be enjoying. Honesty pointed out that I really was having an easier time, but it was far more hazardous than I had envisaged.

There was the problem of dear old John Jenkins, for instance. There was this business of Henry Mawne, whose troubles, I felt in my bones, would one day be brought to my door.

Mrs Pringle was always with me as an irritant, rather like 'the running sore of Europe' one used to hear about in history lessons long ago. Turkey, was it, or France? No, if I remembered rightly 'France's bugbear was a strong and united Germany', so it must have been Turkey that was the 'running sore'.

And then, of course, there was Minnie Pringle, I thought, returning to my list of problems after my historical diversion. It was bad enough having to be on guard against giving her a job in the house in a weak moment, with the train of domestic catastrophes that would entail. Worse still was this new complication of being expected to mediate between Ern and Bert.

'Never come between husband and wife,' had been one of my mother's maxims, along with 'Lazy people take the most pains,' and 'Least said soonest mended.'

I certainly did not intend to become involved in Minnie's matrimonial affairs. Or her extra-marital affairs for that matter.

On the following Wednesday afternoon I duly arrived at Mrs Willet's with my borrowed tape recorder.

Mrs Pringle had eyed it somewhat scornfully as I put it on the back seat, and given a dismissive snort, which I ignored.

Alice Willet had prepared a tray with two teacups and an iced sponge cake large enough to feed a family.

I put the recorder on the table as we refreshed ourselves and assured Alice that I should not switch it on until she gave me permission.

Following Bob's mention of laundry work in her youth I started by asking her to tell me what she remembered. I was surprised at her fluency and memory for detail, and after two minutes switched on with her permission.

From descriptions of the sorting of linen, cotton and similar materials from the woollen ones (no man-made fibres in Mrs Willet's youth), she went on to starching, the use of the blue-bag, turning the heavy mangle by hand, and all the processes that followed.

Within ten minutes I had a wonderful amount of material on laundry work, and she went on, without prompting, to the mending of the freshly ironed clothes and household linen that needed repair.

'Would you like a rest now?' I enquired, but Alice then embarked on the preparations needed in the kitchen before preparing a meal for 'upstairs'. This involved so many technical terms connected with the coal-fired stove, such as 'dampers', that I feared I should have to get expert advice before translating Alice's account for modern readers, and we decided to end our session.

I played it back when I got home, and congratulated myself – and Alice, of course – on having such a wonderful start.

I was still in a state of excitement when Amy called on her way home from Oxford.

'A very good thing that you've found an interest,' she said approvingly, 'but rather a *solitary* occupation, this writing business. I should feel much happier if you *joined things*.'

'But I do,' I protested. 'I belong to Fairacre and Beech Green WIs, and am always buzzing about going to concerts and lectures. And things,' I added rather lamely.

'But it seems so *aimless*,' said my old friend. 'I feel you need to use your mind more. What about politics?'

'What about it?'

'Wouldn't you like to take an active part in helping your local candidate?'

'Frankly, no. And I've had quite enough of meetings and committees and all the rest of 'em while I was teaching. Now I'm enjoying retirement, don't forget, and even so, I get called upon to do jobs I really don't want to do.'

'You did a very good one on updating the pamphlet about the church here,' said Amy generously. 'Isobel Annett told me at the last Choral Society practice.'

'It's with the printers now, I believe,' I said, rather mollified. 'I quite enjoyed that little exercise.'

'Well, you were always good at English at college, so perhaps this little dabbling in old memories will be fulfilling for you.'

'You sound like my doctor,' I observed. 'He doesn't think I'm fulfilled because I haven't had children.'

'You don't want to take any notice of doctors,' said Amy sturdily. 'They get such silly ideas of their importance always being kowtowed to by adoring nurses. It gives them ideas above their station.'

She rose to go.

'By the way, I've promised to raise funds for the Dogs for the Blind some time. I thought a cheese and wine evening perhaps. Makes a change from a coffee morning, and one gets more men if it's a cheese and wine do.'

'I'll come to that with much pleasure. Better still, I'll come over and help you get things ready.'

'Better still,' repeated Amy, 'bring that nice John Jenkins or Henry Mawne. Or both.'

'Not together,' I told her.

Mrs Pringle had heard all about my recording session with Alice Willet, but was pleased to see that the instrument was lying on the kitchen table to be put to use during a prolonged tea interval.

I noticed her smoothing her hair and adjusting her blouse, as I switched on, as if she were facing television cameras.

'Shall I tell you about how my old grandma met her end?' she enquired. 'She had a funny turn coming down the steps at Caxley station, and her legs was —'

'Perhaps something more general,' I broke in. 'About your schooldays in Caxley?'

'Well, they wasn't all that different to things today,' began Mrs Pringle, thwarted of the gruesome account of her grandmother's end. 'Still, I could tell you what I wore when I went to school.'

'Splendid,' I said encouragingly, and she was well away.

'Well, in winter I wore a good woollen vest next to the skin, then a starched cotton chemise, then a petticoat, blouse, woolly cardigan and a pinafore over the lot.'

'Knickers?' I suggested politely.

'Of course,' said Mrs Pringle, bridling. 'Fleecy lined with elastic at waist and legs. In summer I had cotton knickers as fastened on to my Liberty bodice.'

It was surprising how much useful material was obtained at this session. When I came to play it back that evening, I found not only Mrs Pringle's memories of her youthful garments, but some fascinating recollections of old country remedies.

'If we had a stye on the eye, my mum used to rub it with her wedding ring. Had to be pure gold, you see, or it never worked.'

Parson Woodforde, I recalled, writing on the same subject in 1791, had been advised to stroke his stye with the tail of a cat. It had to be a *black* cat, but fortunately he had one handy, and proceeded to stroke the stye with its tail. He found some immediate relief but four days later, he notes 'Eye much inflamed again, and painful,' so presumably the cat's tail was not wholly proficient.

I went to bed that night full of hope for my future project. The next move, I thought, would be to jot down as much as I could remember of dear Dolly Clare's reminiscences. That should give me another few pages, I thought happily, as I settled down to sleep.

My other literary project, the keeping of my personal diary, was not faring so well.

The last entry, for instance, read: 'Washed my new cardigan. It had gone out of shape and the sleeves are now far too long, dammit.' Not, I felt, the sort of thing to match the work of Pepys or Evelyn. It was all rather dispiriting, and the murky January days did not help.

We had a spell of dismal weather, so dark that the lights had to be on all day, and one realized how near the arctic circle our storm-girt island lay. I longed for spring, for sunlight, warmth and flowers.

On just such a gloomy afternoon I was glad to have a visit from John Jenkins, who had called to return a book.

He had also brought me a bowl of early hyacinths, just coming into flower. Nothing could have been more welcome, as I told him.

He enquired after my literary efforts and I brought him up to date, remarking upon my uninspired diary entries.

'Cheer up,' he said kindly, 'at least you're keeping your hand in, and it's your life you are noting, not Pepys' or Evelyn's.'

We sat eating toasted crumpets and sipping tea, and were enjoying each other's company when the telephone rang.

To my surprise, it was Henry. Could he come and see me soon? He'd like to talk things over with me. My heart sank. 'Come to tea tomorrow,' I said, as warmly as I could. 'What's it about?'

There followed a lengthy monologue about his present troubles, Deidre's absence, the possibility of leaving Fairacre, and a touch of sciatica, to add to things.

'But do you think I can help?' I asked doubtfully.

He said that he knew he had been a confounded nuisance in

the past, but he would dearly like a sensible woman's views on his present plight. He sounded sad, but genuinely troubled, and I said I should look forward to seeing him the next day.

'That was Henry,' I told John.

'That man's a menace,' he said, jumping up impatiently, and beginning to pace up and down the room. 'Shall I see him off for you?'

'Why?' I said, suddenly extremely angry.

He turned to look at me, and his face changed.

'I'm sorry,' he said contritely, 'I shouldn't have said that. It's no business of mine.'

'Quite!' I said, still seething.

'It's just that I didn't realize you were so fond of old Henry.'

'I am *not* so fond of old Henry,' I almost shouted, in my exasperation. 'Henry has annoyed me on many occasions, and I think I know his faults as well as you do. However, he's in real trouble and wants my advice, for what it's worth. He's an old friend. He's always been generous to me and the school children. I shall do what I can for him.'

'You put me to shame,' said John. 'I'm sorry I've upset you. Perhaps I'd better go.'

'Oh, don't be a *chump*,' I said wearily. 'Sit down and have another cup of tea. We're not going to have a row about Henry.'

He resumed his seat. For the first time he looked thoroughly discomfited, and I liked him all the better for it.

'I should know better than to interfere in your private affairs,' he said. 'It's just that I'm so fond of you I hate to see you being bothered by anybody.'

'Point taken,' I replied lightly, and let him have the last crumpet.

10 Henry's Troubles

O F COURSE, I spent that night, the next morning and early afternoon pondering on the coming interview with Henry Mawne.

All that I had said to John during my outburst was quite true. Henry had been the source of much embarrassment to me over the years, but he was a decent man, I liked him, and I was very sorry for him at the moment.

On the other hand, all my mother's warnings about interfering in married couples' affairs, came back to me and, in any case, I certainly did not want to encourage Henry to come and pour out his heart whenever he felt inclined.

I thought he had aged a lot when he arrived, and soon supplied him with that panacea for all ills mental and physical, a cup of tea. It crossed my mind, as I handed it to him, that Amy would be delighted to know that I had company. My own unworthy thought was, should I ever have my house to myself?

He seemed unable to broach the subject of his unhappiness, and in the end I took the bull by the horns and said:

'Well, fire away, Henry. I am truly sorry about your present affairs. Can I help?'

'It really all depends on Deidre,' he began, crumbling a

piece of shortbread in a rather messy fashion, so that a goodly proportion was strewn on the hearth rug.

'She's still in Ireland, I suppose?'

'Yes, and likely to stay there. I don't blame her. She never really settled in Fairacre. But she is really being most difficult.'

I began to wonder if poor Deidre was going to be blamed for Henry's misfortunes in her absence. It rather complicated the issue for me as adviser.

'So what's the position?'

'She's determined to stay in Ireland, and I shall have to go there to live if I want to save the marriage.'

'And do you?'

Henry looked startled.

'Do I want to save my marriage?' he queried, sounding amazed at such a question. 'Of course I do! Deidre may be rather a handful at the moment, but I love her very much. Besides, we made a contract to keep to each other for better or worse, so long as we both should live. Can't go back on a promise like that!'

'Plenty do.'

'Maybe,' said Henry. 'I don't.'

At least one point was clear and I was not going to be called upon to come between husband and wife.

'Will you mind living in Ireland?'

'Not a bit. Lovely country, know quite a few people there, and the gardens do well.'

'So what's the problem between you both?'

'I suppose I tried too hard to get her to come back here. I really have put down roots in Fairacre, and I love the old house and garden. But she was so obstinate about it I lost my temper pretty often, and then she'd flit off to stay with friends and leave me "to stew in my own juice", as she used to say.'

'Have you been in touch since you've been back? Does she know you are willing to go back to Ireland?'

Henry looked doubtful.

'Well, I've written several times, but she doesn't read letters, and often doesn't answer the phone. I think I shall simply go back and tell her.'

'Have you got somewhere there to live?'

'That's the snag. She still owns – or rather rents – a tumble-down Irish cabin in County Mayo. We couldn't live there permanently, but I haven't enough cash to buy a suitable place until I've sold my own here. You know, I expect, that it's on the market?'

I said that I had heard. I did not like to say that I had been acquainted of this news long before the advertisement had appeared in the *Caxley Chronicle*, and from several informants, but Henry knew village ways as well as I did, so I kept quiet.

'What do you think I should do?' enquired Henry, looking helpless.

'You must tell Deidre what you have just told me, that you want a happy marriage and you are content to live in Ireland. Write and telephone as well, and if you don't hear from her you will have to get a go-between.'

'A go-between?' echoed Henry. 'One of those marriage guidance blokes, or counsellors, or whatever they call themselves? Not likely!'

He had turned quite pink with indignation, and I hastened to explain.

'No, no! I meant an old friend of you both whose judgement you valued. Or your solicitor. Someone like that who would explain things to Deidre if you hadn't been able to hear from her.'

Henry seemed relieved.

'Oh, our solicitor is just the chap over there. He was at

kindergarten with Deidre, and we go fishing together. Can't think why I never thought of him before.'

'But do try Deidre first,' I said hastily. 'And tell her you've put the house up for sale. It will show her you are really serious.'

'It's not going to be easy to sell. Wants a lot doing to it. Still, it's a nice place, and I'd like to see it go as a family house. Gerald Partridge seemed to think that some institution like Distressed Gentlefolk or Delinquent Boys might be interested.'

'Not to *share*, I trust. The Gentlefolk would soon be even more Distressed with Delinquent Boys under the same roof.'

Henry ignored my flippancy. He was looking at me with great solemnity.

'You wouldn't feel like going over to explain things to Deidre yourself, would you?'

'Definitely not!' I said firmly. 'Now, you write to Deidre this evening, and try to get her on the telephone, and if you haven't heard anything by early next week, then ring your solicitor and tell him to get on to Deidre urgently.'

'I suppose you're right,' agreed Henry, glancing at the clock. 'Well, I'd best get back. If I write tonight it should get the first post.'

He rose, and made for the door. There he turned.

'You are a dear girl,' he said. 'Helped me a lot.'

'Not really,' I said. 'You'd already worked it out.'

I opened the front door.

'See much of John Jenkins?' he said suddenly.

'Quite a bit.'

'Good! He's a thoroughly nice chap. He'd take good care of you. Always liked him.'

He strode off briskly to his car, and I returned to the fireside, pondering his comments on John.

Comparisons are odious, we all know, but in this instance

Henry appeared in a more favourable light than his old school friend who had spoken so disparagingly of him at our last encounter.

I carried the tea things to the kitchen, and returned with a dustpan and brush to clear up the remains of Henry's meal from the hearth rug.

I woke next morning with the comforting thought that there was absolutely nothing in the diary to upset my day, and also that it was the frst of February, and surely Spring must come soon?

I promised myself a solitary walk in the woods nearby, and a leisurely potter in the garden sometime during the day. With any luck I might find that '*Peace came dripping slow*', as W. B. Yeats put it. It was high time it did, I thought.

It was wonderfully quiet in the little copse some hundred yards from my home. Only the rustle of dead leaves under my

feet and the throbbing of a wood pigeon's monotonous song above disturbed the silence.

I sat on a handy log and surveyed the scene. It was still a winter one, with bare trees and little foliage apart from two sturdy fir trees which must have provided welcome shelter to the birds during the storms.

But there were small signs of spring. The shafts of sunlight sloping through the trees provided some warmth, and near at hand the wild honeysuckle, which twined about the trunk of a young beech tree, was already showing a few tiny leaves, 'no bigger than a mouse's ear', as I had read somewhere.

On moving the dead leaves with my muddy boot, I un-earthed the small shiny upsproutings of some bluebells which, in a few months' time, would be transforming the scene into a mist of blue and filling the wood with heady fragrance.

I picked a sprig of the honeysuckle to take home as a fore-runner of spring, and half an hour later I put it in a glass specimen vase to stand beside John Jenkins' pink hyacinths, now at their best.

Much refreshed in spirit, I set about a pile of ironing which had been awaiting attention for far too long, and then resumed my outdoor wanderings around the garden.

It was showing hopeful signs of spring too. Already the early miniature irises, yellow and blue, were showing colour, and a viburnum had broken into leaf.

There was a good deal of bird activity in the hedges, and I guessed that nest-building had already begun. Altogether I had a delightfully refreshing day of solitude, and it was seven o'clock before the telephone rang. Luckily, it was Amy.

'Do you know,' I told her, 'you are the first person I have spoken to today.'

'Good heavens,' cried Amy, sounding shocked, 'how

dreadful for you! If only I'd known, I should have asked you here.'

I tried to explain that I had thoroughly enjoyed my day after rather a lot of visitors, but Amy could not understand it.

'I assure you, it's been like Paddington Station here the last few days,' I said, and told her about Henry's troubles.

'I think you've been very patient with him,' she said at last. 'He must be a rather silly man.'

'He's unhappy.'

'Well, I expect it's six of one and half a dozen of the other,' said Amy philosophically. 'They must sort it out together. You've done your bit admirably, I'd say.'

I felt quite flattered. Amy seldom praises me.

'It's about my proposed wine and cheese party,' she went on. 'The "Dogs for the Blind" do, I spoke about.'

'The children of Fairacre always called it "Blind Dogs",' I told her. 'They used to bring masses of silver paper for blind dogs. I can't think what they imagined the poor animals would do with it.'

'Didn't you explain?'

'Of course I did, but it went in one ear and out the other, I expect.'

'I know, I know,' said Amy sympathetically. 'Well, the point is that I must postpone the idea. James has a conference in Cyprus soon, and he wants me to go with him. I must say the thought of some sunshine attracts me, and as the dates I had thought of have already been snaffled by the local National Trust and the League of Pity, I'm bowing out until later in the year.'

'Fair enough. Count on me for help when the time comes.'

'Thank you, darling. And how's John Jenkins?'

'Very well,' I said guardedly.

'I gather he may be giving up his house in France,' said Amy.

'Friends of ours use the same agent over there. They know John slightly.'

'Oh? I hadn't heard anything about it.'

'Just a rumour, I expect,' said Amy lightly. 'You know how things get about.'

'I certainly do!' I said with conviction, and we rang off.

When Mrs Pringle arrived on Wednesday afternoon, it was obvious that she was bursting with news.

'You heard about our Minnie?' she asked. I felt my usual alarm at the mention of Minnie.

'Don't say she wants to call here,' I said.

'No, no! Nothing like that. But her Ern's run off.'

'Good heavens! It's usually the other way. Who with?'

Mrs Pringle bridled, and I felt that I had made a gaffe.

'With nobody! Just run off. Back to his ma, I expect. And he won't be welcomed there, that's for sure.'

I remembered Mrs Pringle telling me once of Ern's mother's high principles and her stern ways with malefactors, particularly those related to her.

'But surely she will send him back to Minnie?'

'That's the trouble. You see, Bert's moved in with her.'

Bert is one of Minnie's long-term admirers, and has caused more trouble than anyone in that storm-torn household.

'He must be mad!' I exclaimed.

A maudlin look came over Mrs Pringle's dour countenance.

'That's true. Mad with *love*!' she said, almost simpering.

There is a streak of sickly sentimentality in Mrs Pringle's otherwise flinty make-up, which never ceases to dumbfound me.

'But Bert must know he is making trouble,' I protested.

'He don't see it that way. He just wants to be with the woman he loves.'

I gave up. Minnie, Bert and Ern must get on with their own muddles. Let them stew in their own juice.

'Of course, if you'd like to have a word with Bert,' began Mrs Pringle, but I cut her short.

'No!' I said, fortissimo.

'In that case,' she replied, 'I'll Flash the bathroom.'

She made for the stairs. Her limp, I noticed, was marked.

Later that day Bob Willet cycled over from Fairacre, ostensibly to return a cookery book I had lent to Alice, but really, I guessed, because he needed company.

We sat by the fire with a glass of wine apiece, and Bob told me all the news.

'Heard about Minnie?'

I said I had.

'Don't blame Ern for slinging his hook, but that Bert wants his head seen to.'

I agreed.

'Mind you,' he went on, 'Bert is a useless article altogether. He's supposed to be a painter and decorator, but Mr Mawne had him in to do the doors and windows, and a proper pig's breakfast he made of it.'

I was secretly glad to hear of Henry, and rather hoped that Bob would tell me more.

'Bert with a paint brush,' continued Bob, 'was like a cow with a musket. I told Mr Mawne, on the quiet, to give him the sack. I could've done better myself, and I don't reckon to be a painter.'

He put down his glass and looked at the clock.

'Am I in your way?'

I reassured him on this point.

'Well, my Alice won't be back for an hour or so.'

I refilled his glass.

'Hey, watch it!' he protested. 'I'll be falling off my bike.'

'Well, you won't be breathalyzed.'

'That's true. Mr Mawne was the other night, but sober as a judge, so that was lucky. He still hasn't sold the house, you know.'

'So I gather.'

'It's not everyone's cup of tea.'

'Rather large, but someone might buy it as an investment.'

'Rather them than me,' said Bob stoutly, rising to his feet. 'I'd best be off before you gets me too tiddly.'

I watched him set off. He seemed as steady as ever on his ancient bicycle, and I returned to the fireside wondering once more about Henry Mawne's future.

11 A Fresh Idea

Signs of spring grew thick and fast, lifting our spirits after January's gloom. The miniature yellow irises blazed in a sheltered corner, the first leaves of the bulbs were pushing through, and the horse-chestnut gleamed with sticky buds.

Two blackbirds were busy making a nest in the lilac bush near the gate, watched by Tibby with great interest.

But perhaps the most cheering sign was the lengthening days. I remembered Dolly Clare saying how she welcomed February, 'because you could have a walk in the light after tea'. From such little things does spring begin.

Some days after Bob Willet's visit, I had a telephone call from Henry Mawne. He sounded in his more usual, buoyant mood, and I felt relieved.

Evidently he had had some trouble in tracking down his elusive wife, but had taken my advice and got in touch with the solicitor friend who knew where she was staying at the time.

'Luckily, she answered the phone,' said Henry, 'and I must say was very sweet and helpful about everything. I'm flying over tomorrow, and that's why I'm ringing now. You were such a tower of strength, and I want to keep you in the picture.'

I must say that it was nice to hear that I had been a tower of strength. I must remember to tell Amy sometime, I decided.

'Did you mention the house?' I asked.

'Which one?'

'Yours, of course. Is there any other?'

'Oh! *My house* here, you mean? Yes, I told her it was up for sale. She was pleased about that.'

I thought he sounded a little hurt at Deidre's reaction.

'I do mind a bit about it, you know,' he said, as if he had guessed my thoughts. 'If I had the money to put it right, I

think I'd have gone on with my efforts to persuade Deidre to stay here.'

Privately, I thought it would have been banging his head against a brick wall, but I voiced my thoughts more kindly.

'Well, you tried, Henry, heaven knows, and you got nowhere by sticking to your guns like that. In fact, it may have made Deidre more decided, as it happened. I'm sure you are doing the right thing to put your marriage first.'

Whether he had been listening to my words of wisdom, I don't know, but his next remark was about another house.

'Deidre's been looking out for somewhere to live over there. That's why I was in a muddle when you mentioned a house. No hope yet, but property's not so expensive there, so with luck, the sale of the Fairacre one should provide something Deidre likes. And where she wants it, of course, which is the main object.'

'Well, good luck with it all, Henry,' I said, rather anxious to end the conversation, as Tibby had just walked in holding a writhing mouse.

'I'll be in touch from Ireland,' he assured me.

I put down the receiver to attend to more immediate problems. Tibby was not amused.

I had not seen John Jenkins since our little tiff about Henry's affairs, but he had rung once or twice, and I knew he was busy with something to do with Uncle Sam's affairs.

As a young man Uncle Sam had put money into some farming project in South America. It had not proved very lucrative, but now that he was dead there was a certain amount of clearing up to do, and the authorities over there were remarkably difficult to pin down, according to Uncle Sam's solicitor.

'As far as I can see,' John had told me, 'there will be nothing coming in from all these tedious negotiations but a hefty bill from the legal eagles on both sides of the Atlantic. I'm just letting them get on with it.'

He ended the conversation in the routine way by asking me to marry him. I expressed my usual appreciation of the honour he had done me and refused yet again.

Sometimes I wondered what he would do if I said 'Yes'.

But I did not intend to try it.

The wind got up on the night that Henry had rung me. The windows shuddered in the onslaught, and clouds scudded across the face of the full moon.

The winter-bare branches of the copper beech tree waved wildly this way and that, and the roaring of the gale made sleep impossible.

I went downstairs to make a cup of tea. It was the sort of night when roof tiles slid off, and chimney pots hurtled to the ground. I hoped that Henry's roof would stand up to the rigours of the wind, and was glad that I had a snug thatch to protect me.

It was quieter in the kitchen at the back of the house, and I sat at the table with my tea and hoped that the gale would blow itself out before poor old Henry set off.

At least he would be flying, and not have to face hours on that notoriously choppy crossing from England to Ireland.

But I was apprehensive for Henry's future, although it was really none of my business. My opinion of him had risen considerably since our talk about his problems. I thought that he was tackling them with wisdom, patience and courage. I only hoped that Deidre would continue to co-operate as she seemed to have done when Henry had at last tracked her down.

Although I liked Deidre, I suspected that her feelings and her loyalties were nowhere near as firmly rooted as Henry's. She was a light-weight. She was wayward and spoilt. Would she lead Henry a dance when she had him back, or would they be able to settle down, I wondered? Well, no good speculating, I told myself, draining my cup.

I went to bed again, and slept like the dead, oblivious of the raging storm around me.

The rough weather continued for several days, and when Mrs Pringle arrived the next Wednesday 'to bottom me', she was wind-blown and breathless.

'I was nearly flung to the ground waiting for the Caxley,' she told me. 'Tossed about like a leaf.'

I tried to envisage Mrs Pringle as a twelve-stone leaf, but failed.

'Plays my leg up real cruel,' she went on, 'and Fred's got his chest again.'

I bit back the query as to where Fred's chest had been, and helped her off with her coat.

'You'd better sit down,' I said, 'before making a start.'

She lowered herself heavily into a chair, and sighed.

'I told you about Ern, didn't I?'

I said that yes, indeed she had, and was everything settled now?

A look of intense satisfaction spread across her face.

'Thanks to Ern's mum, everything's fine.'

'Good,' I said, waiting expectantly.

'It's like this. As you know, Ern's mum has got a nice little corner shop in Caxley, and a flat above it. Savings too, she's got, so Ern thinks, and as he's the only child he reckons he'll come into it all.'

'And will he? I had an idea she had threatened to cut him out of her will some time ago because of his behaviour.'

'That's right. She did *threaten*, but never actually done it. But this time she took a stronger line. No sooner had he turned up, when she told him that he was to take her to Springbourne and she'd sort things out.'

'But Bert was there surely? Wasn't that rather rash?'

'You don't know Ern's mother. If ever there was a Christian soldier it was her. Right's right and wrong's wrong to her, and she told Ern he had duties as a husband and father, and he was just to get back home and do them.'

I began to feel the greatest respect for Ern's mother. If ever she decided to stand for Parliament, she would have my vote.

'Go on, what happened?'

'Well, knowing as that will of hers was going to be altered the very next morning, of course Ern had to take her back in the van. She took her husband's old gun with her too. Not loaded, of course, but she wasn't above giving Bert – or Ern, for that matter – a clump on the head with it.'

The kitchen clock ticked on as Mrs Pringle's narrative continued, but I decided the housework took second place this afternoon.

It appeared that as soon as the van pulled up and Ern's redoubtable mother emerged with the gun, Minnie Pringle set up the sort of hysterical screaming that engages the attention of all within earshot.

Consequently, interested neighbours appeared in their front gardens, or at open windows, the better to take part in the drama.

It was a swift victory. As the raiding party, Ern and his mother, stormed up the front path, Bert ignominiously burst

from the back door, leapt the privet hedge and ran across the field of turnips to take cover in a nearby wood.

Minnie, still yelling, opened the front door, two toddlers clinging to her skirt, to let in her husband and mother-in-law, who carried the gun pointing before her.

The onlookers had the exquisite pleasure of seeing Ern's mother prop the weapon by the umbrella stand with one hand and administer a sharp slap to Minnie's face with the other, before the front door was slammed shut, and the noise of the battle ceased.

'She told me,' said Mrs Pringle, 'that this was the last straw, and she told Minnie and Ern that if she heard another squeak out of them or out of Bert, her shop and the flat and her savings in the Caxley Building Society was all going to the Salvation Army. She's always been a great supporter of that, and Ern knows it.'

It seemed right to me that such a militant Christian should leave her resources to such a good cause, and said so.

'She will too,' said Mrs Pringle, struggling to her feet. 'I think she's settled their hash properly this time. Gave them a good fright.'

'What about Bert?'

'If my Minnie's got any sense, and mind you, she hasn't got much, as we well know, she'll keep Bert at bay, if he's silly enough to worry her again.'

She looked at the clock.

'Is that the time? Well, if you will keep me gossiping here, I shall just have to leave the brights till next Wednesday, and do the usual and leave it at that.'

I felt that the postponement of attention to the copper and brass objects in my establishment was a small price to pay for being brought up to date in the stormy history of Minnie's matrimonial affairs.

As we drove home after her labours, Mrs Pringle asked how my work on old memories was progressing, and I was obliged to tell her that I was not getting on very fast.

The project, I had to admit to myself, for some time now, was not very satisfactory.

Apart from Mrs Pringle's contribution and that of Mrs Willet, there were very few sources, I discovered.

I had jotted down those memories of Dolly Clare's which I could recall, but she would have supplied a wealth of material.

Dear old Doctor Martin who had been in practice when I first came to Fairacre, and Miss Parr who had lived at Henry Mawne's house in my early days, were dead.

The vicar had said that he would do his best to recall anything that might be of interest, but frankly, I did not think the material he could offer would be particularly interesting.

I discussed my problem with John, who had read all my efforts and given me much encouragement. He was also somewhat critical, so that I was alternately flattered and dismayed.

'I think this trivial sort of thing is getting you nowhere,' he announced. 'You say yourself that you'll never get enough useful material together to make a book. What else can you do with it?'

I told him that I had broached the possibility of an article or two in the *Caxley Chronicle* with the editor.

'And what did he say?'

'He was diplomatic, but decidedly daunting. He said they had masses of similar material, and suggested I might like to use some of my stuff for 'corner-fillers' on their 'Local Memories' page. You know, 'How Grandmother Cured her Chilblains' in two hundred and fifty words. I don't want that.'

'I should hope not.'

John looked at me steadily.

'You know you write extremely well. Forget this fiddling about and start a proper book.'

I looked at him in horror.

'A book? A novel, do you mean? I haven't a clue about thinking up a plot, to begin with!'

'You could do it,' he said decisively. 'That is if you really do want to carry on with this writing idea. What made you start anyway?'

I tried to explain about my restlessness after that week of teaching again at Fairacre school, and he listened patiently.

'I think that simply brought things to a head,' he said at last. 'You were full of euphoria when you first started retirement, revelling in having time to yourself and so on, and then this spell of teaching just made you realize that you needed something more from life than just mooning about in the fields and woods.'

'I don't care for that expression "mooning about"', I told him. 'You make me sound like some loony old witch.'

He ignored my interruption and continued.

'And you're right, of course. You're much too bright to find complete satisfaction in domestic matters.'

'Thank you,' I said, somewhat mollified.

'On the other hand,' he went on, now well away in analysing my problems, much to my amusement and some surprise, 'you're not the sort of person who wants to play bridge or golf, or join a lot of clubs where you meet hordes of people. That I can well understand.'

'So what do you suggest, dear Agony Uncle?'

'Well, you could marry me, and find enormous satisfaction in looking after me. It would be a very noble aim, and much appreciated.'

'Nothing doing, John.'

'So I feared. But that aside, I do think something like writing, which you could do in the solitude you like so much, might be just the thing for you.'

He looked so earnest that I got up and kissed the top of his head. He really had the most attractive silvery hair I had ever seen on a man.

'What's that for?' he asked, looking up.

'To thank you for all your kind concern, and as I was passing to put on the kettle, I gave you a friendly kiss.'

'You couldn't make it more passionate?'

'Not until we've had our coffee,' I told him, going into the kitchen.

After John had gone, I thought about his ideas for my future. I was much touched by his concern for my happiness, and wished I loved him enough to marry him. What a simple solution that would be!

His final words about my proposed literary career had been spoken as we walked down the path to his car.

'You know, I couldn't possibly write a novel,' I protested.

'No one asked you to. It was your crazy idea to write a novel. All I think is that you should write about something you know.'

'But I don't know anything.'

He stopped to unlock the car door, and then straightened up.

'You know all about being a village schoolmistress for years. You could start on that.'

He waved to George Annett who was wobbling by on his bicycle, and then got into the driving seat.

'I'll give you a word-processor for your birthday,' he promised, and drove away, leaving me to mull over all his plans for my future employment.

It was good of him to take so much interest, I thought, as I went about my affairs during the next few days, and I was intrigued by his insight into my character.

He was quite right about my dislike of joining things that would mean meeting lots of people. Amy was not nearly so perceptive, although she had known me far longer.

I remembered her horror when I had told her that I had been alone all day. To Amy solitude was anathema. To me it was vital, at least for part of my day. John had recognized that. He had also realized that domestic duties would not satisfy me. Of course, it might have been a polite way of excusing my house-keeping shortcomings. Perhaps he thought me a proper slut? Compared with his own immaculate house I supposed mine might look rather a mess, despite Mrs Pringle's weekly attentions. It was a chastening thought.

I decided to put aside all these problems. After all, I had come to terms now with my retirement. Despite John's assessment of my needs, I was slightly less restless than I had been after my unsettling week at Fairacre school, but maybe I did need some central interest which I could pursue at my own pace and in the quietness I preferred.

I would think about it. Thankfully my health seemed to be restored after what Mrs Pringle called 'my funny turn', actually a slight stroke.

I had good health, a dear little house and, even more precious, a host of friends.

These things spelt happiness.

12   Looking Ahead

Henry Mawne was as good as his word, and I had a long conversation with him one evening on the telephone.

He sounded happy and said that he and Deidre had been busy searching for a house that they both liked and could afford.

'Any luck?'

'Well, we've looked at everything from one-roomed cabins you wouldn't keep your chickens in, to crumbling castles, but I think we've whittled it down to a couple of farm houses. They've both got enough fields to keep horses for Deidre.'

'I'd no idea she wanted horses,' I said, somewhat shocked.

'Oh, everyone keeps horses in Ireland,' said Henry airily. 'Just as we keep an old bike in the garden shed.'

'And are prices high over there?'

'Less than ours, which is a good thing. And the great news is that the Caxley agent has had an offer for the Fairacre one.'

'Well, that's marvellous! Will you take it?'

'It's not the asking price, of course, but I hardly expected that. But it's a very fair offer and I shall certainly accept it.'

'Who is it?'

'No idea. The agent didn't say. I'll know before long, I expect.'

He asked after his Fairacre friends, told me that he would be writing to the vicar about a discrepancy he had found in the church accounts, and we rang off with mutual expressions of affection to all and sundry.

I was delighted to know that all was going well, and hoped to hear more about the purchaser of Henry's property when I met Mrs Pringle or Bob Willet or Mr Lamb in the near future.

To my surprise, Mrs Pringle knew nothing about it, but hinted darkly about *developers* who more than likely would raze Henry's home to the ground and put up a couple of dozen rabbit hutches on the site in which you couldn't swing a cat should you so wish.

Bob Willet was no more help, and Mr Lamb had heard it was 'some old gent who was now past driving and wanted to be within walking distance of the shop and the church and that.'

With these unsatisfactory snippets I had to be content, but knowing village life I felt that I should soon learn all.

Spring seemed lovelier than ever this year. The early daffodils had 'come before the swallow dared', and lit the garden with their brightness.

The growing warmth lured me into the garden, and all sorts of indoor duties such as turning out cupboards, sending loose covers to the cleaners and polishing the windows, simply went by the board.

One sunny morning I was busy weeding at the end of the garden, watched by Tibby lolling nearby, when I thought I heard somebody at the front door, and went to investigate.

I found John trying to stuff a large envelope through the letter-box.

'Hello,' I said. 'You'd better let me have that before my letter-box snaps your fingers off. What is it?'

'Open it and see,' he said.

'Well, come and sit in the garden,' I said, pulling off my muddy gloves.

We sat side by side on my new garden seat. I ripped open the envelope. Inside were two things. One was an exercise book, and the other a long box containing a splendid pen.

'John,' I exclaimed with delight, 'this is the pen the opera stars use in the advertisements.'

'And the top footballers,' added John.

I turned to the exercise book. It was one of those nice old-fashioned ones with multiplication tables on the back, and the useful rhyme about the days in each month.

'Heavens! How this takes me back,' I cried. 'How clever of you.'

'It's really to start you moving with that book of yours,' he confessed. 'I thought you'd be more at home with a pen and exercise book, and once you're well away I'll add the word processor.'

'I'll have a go,' I promised him. I began to feel quite excited at the prospect.

'Good girl!' he said, stretching out his long legs and turning his face to the sun.

'Let's go out for lunch,' he added. 'What about that nice pub we visited once when we were going to Stratford? The White Hart, or The Red Lion, or some coloured animal.'

'You don't mean The Blue Boar?'

'No. It was up on the downs. We went through Spring-bourne to it. They always do bubble-and-squeak.'

I racked my brain for more coloured-animal pubs which did bubble-and-squeak, but drew a blank.

'Do you mean The Woodman?'

'That's right. Let's go there.'

'I'd love to. Coffee first, or go now?'

He looked at his watch.

'Let's go now while the sun's out. We'll get a marvellous view from the top of the downs.'

The sun was high as we got out of the car, and walked on the springy turf to a handy five-barred gate nearby.

The view was indeed marvellous. The village of Fairacre could be seen below us to the left, and Springbourne to the right, two small settlements dwarfed by the great fields about them.

'That reminds me,' I said. 'I had a call from Henry a day or two ago.'

'How is the old boy?'

'He sounds more hopeful. Deidre is being co-operative at the moment and they are busy looking for a house. Thank goodness that after all this time he has had an offer for his Fairacre place.'

John's answer astounded me.

'I know. I made the offer.'

When I had got my breath back, I bombarded him with questions.

'But why? Why go to Henry's house when you have a much nicer one in Beech Green? Do you mean to leave that one?'

John turned round from the gate and leant his back on it. He looked amused.

'No, I do not intend to leave the house in Beech Green, at least for some time.'

'Well, that's a relief! I should miss you terribly. But why buy Henry's?'

'Come back to the car and I'll tell you. This downland air is very invigorating but a trifle parky, I find.'

'It's like this,' said John, as we trundled gently away towards bubble-and-squeak. 'I'm looking to the future. There's going to come a time when my staircase at the cottage is going to be a problem. It's steep and twisty. Added to that, I have to get out the car every time I need anything. In my old age I shall want a ground floor flat within walking distance of the village shop and the church, not to mention neighbours nearby.'

I suddenly remembered Mr Lamb's comment about 'the old gent who was past driving,' and began to laugh.

'What's the joke?'

I told him.

'Well, as you see, he's just about right,' was his comment.

I was still perplexed.

'But can you afford to run two homes, John? I believe Henry's place needs a lot doing to it.'

'It certainly does,' he agreed. 'But luckily I've sold my place in France. I've got past coping with the drive down, or even hanging about at airports. I'm now shortening all my lines of communication.'

By this time we had arrived at The Woodman, but we sat in the car outside to continue the story.

'Also I had the chance to sell my share of Uncle Sam's holding in that South American farming project. Some distant cousin, twenty-five times removed, has taken it on, which should bring me in something. When, heaven knows, but I'm keeping my fingers crossed.'

'You seem to have been very business-like, and I'm so relieved you are staying in Beech Green.'

'I shan't go until I'm absolutely decrepit, but I've always liked Fairacre more than Beech Green, and that house of Henry's is a gem. I shall enjoy doing it up. Besides, it's going to be my source of income in the future. I could make three first-class flats out of it and they should bring in quite a bit. I shall have a lovely ground floor one to share with you as soon as you say the word.'

I began to laugh.

'Is that today's proposal?'

'Of course. And I forgot to say that dear old Uncle Sam's effects have been sold at quite incredibly high prices, and I have the proceeds. So can I invite you to share a dish of bubble-and-squeak?'

'Indeed you can,' I assured him, as we emerged from the car.

There was plenty to think about in the next few days. I was much impressed by John's efficiency and the way he was facing the future.

If things worked out as he hoped then he would have a pleasant and rewarding time ahead putting Henry's house in order. He had asked me to help him with advice, and this I looked forward to doing. It was good to know that he had done his old schoolfellow a good turn when Henry had been in a difficult situation. Henry had always expressed his admiration of John to me, but it was John who had, until now, been somewhat dismissive and derogatory about Henry.

I did not like to think of myself as the woman in the case, but there was no doubt about it that once Deidre appeared again on the scene John's attitude had become less aggressive towards Henry.

In any case, they must get on with it, I thought, and maybe in the light of these new developments peace and harmony would be restored.

I had put John's exercise book on the dresser to remind me of my promise to him 'to have a go', but the days passed, and I found myself feeling more guilty daily.

If I were to take his advice and write my own memoirs as a village schoolmistress, I ought to think of a title, I told myself. This, of course, kept me from the dreaded moment of writing on the first blank page of my exercise book.

What about *Memories of a Village Schoolteacher*? Too dull, I decided. Or perhaps *Rooks Above the Playground*? Too fanciful, I thought. *Country Children*? *The Heart of the Village*? Somehow none seemed right.

I did actually sit down at the kitchen table one morning and open the exercise book. I sat staring at the virgin page in a state of gloom. Surely, all books should begin with an arresting opening which would lead the reader on to pursue the two or three hundred printed pages with rapture.

At that moment Amy had rung me, and I put the book back thankfully on the dresser.

She was delighted to hear about John's present and my future literary success, and promised to buy a dozen copies for Christmas presents.

Mrs Pringle, on Wednesday afternoon, was less enthusiastic. She picked up the book by its corner, as if it were something highly contagious, and asked what I was doing with it?

I said, with some hauteur, that I proposed to write in it one day. She sniffed, and limped away.

The book began to haunt me. To put it out of sight in a drawer seemed like admitting defeat, so it stayed on the dresser and gave me a twinge of conscience every time I passed it.

A week or two after our lunch at The Woodman, John picked it up and looked inside. I felt like a child caught with a spoon in the honey pot.

'My darling girl,' he cried, 'you haven't written one word!'

He looked so disappointed I could have wept. He brushed aside my feeble excuses with his customary kindness.

'Good lord!' he said briskly. 'Don't let it bother you. If I thought you would worry I shouldn't have given you the things. Put 'em in the dustbin, and forget all about it.'

He changed the subject by telling me that all was going ahead steadily with the purchase of his new house, and that he and Henry had had a long telephone conversation, to their mutual satisfaction. Better still, Deidre was being the perfect wife, and they had started their own negotiations for the farm-house of her choice.

'They hoped,' he added, 'to see us over there when they had got settled.'

As he went, he picked up the exercise book.

'Shall I dispose of it for you?' he asked. 'I'm not going to see you worrying about the wretched thing.'

'No!' I said with sudden strength. 'Leave it there. I may get inspired some time.'

It was obvious, I thought, as I waved him goodbye, that I was going to get involved in other people's affairs, as well as my own, during my peaceful retirement.

*

Three days later, I came in from 'mooning about the fields and woods' as John had once described my walks.

The early evening sunlight had fallen across the neglected exercise book, and seemed to exert a stronger influence than ever. I sat at the kitchen table, and opened it. I reviewed again the half dozen or so titles which had occurred to me over the weeks. Somehow they all seemed pretty trite, and I could not see hordes of eager readers flocking to the booksellers to buy it.

I turned resolutely from this dispiriting thought. After all, one did not need to have the title until the book was written. In fact, it would probably be best to see how it turned out before labelling it.

I picked up John's lovely pen. A vision of his disappointed face, as he had seen my empty exercise book, floated before me.

I pulled the book before me, refusing to be daunted by that virgin page, and all the others which followed it.

On the top line I wrote: CHAPTER ONE, and felt marvellous.

At last, I had made a start.